M.A.D.

by Charles Howard Spring

For Joshua Murray

You are deeply missed.

Chapter 1

Isaac ran over the text of code on the screen one last time. He didn't think he could make any more perfections to the design.

He, Isaac Torre, brilliant scientist and professional nerd, had been assigned perhaps the most dangerous mission he had ever had. He was to create a series of machines that were to defend the Terra colony from the attacks of the alien invaders from space.
The machines they had found from alien wreckage had provided the majority of the information that Isaac had been using. As it turned out, the machines themselves used improvised weaponry to fuel attacks and energy.
For example, the jets had used the power of the air they flew through to create energy bursts and fire cannons for their attacks on the mainland of earth. Isaac had been pushing the bounds of his knowledge of physics and science to create...

SLAM!
Isaac jumped.
"DR. TORRE!" a man yelled from behind him. "Is it ready?"
Isaac stood up and straightened his lab coat. Turning around, Captain Glenn Orvis stood at the door to his lab looking impatient.
I can't say that I blame him, Isaac thought.
The Captain of the Terra colony stood there in his black uniform. Though he was a man in his late 50's, his silver hair was

not meant to take away from his stature. Glenn stared down any people who would oppose him and his leadership. All those who lived in the colony trusted him with their lives.

"I'm just putting the finishing touches on it," Isaac said quickly. He turned back around in his chair. "I was just going to run the final tests on the mechanical systems of the..."

"We don't have time for that! The next attack could occur at any moment!" Glenn roared, stepping over to him. "Our gun torrents can't handle any more of these waves upon waves of enemy attack!"

The gun torrents, Isaac thought. When the colony was created, Gun torrents were placed all around the sphere of the giant dome-like structure (in fact, most of the colony was inside a mountain). The alien invaders had attacked the colony many, many times over the past month or so. Damage had been sustained to the outer shell of the colony. Though it was reinforced with steel, it was not going to last forever. And, while repairs had been made, the constant attacks by the alien invaders made planning and maintaining such repairs difficult. They needed a more permanent way to fend them off.

That was where Isaac came in.

"Also," Captain Orvis told him, "Our candidate has arrived. Mr. Hall, bring him in."

At the door of the laboratory, two men entered. One of them was a tall, thin and yet muscular man wearing green military fatigues.

The one next to him wore not green, but gray. He had been adorned in a gray jumpsuit with the red letters M.A.D. on the chest. Down the sides, extending down the legs was a pair of red stripes.

"Dr. Torre, I'd like you to meet John Rylund," Captain Orvis told him.

John was a tall, broad chested man with brown hair and hazel eyes. Isaac had never met him personally – his duties with the project kept him absent from the selection process.

"Mr. Rylund," Captain Orvis said. "This is Dr. Isaac Torre, he has been working on the new arsenal for the colony's defense."

"Pleased to meet you, Mr. Rylund," Isaac said, standing up again.

Shaking his hand firmly, John replied, "Likewise, Dr. Torre." Then he added: "Am I to thank you for this outfit I'm in?"

Isaac couldn't resist a smile. "Yes, and please just call me Isaac..."

He glanced at Captain Orvis. The Captain had him under a stern glare.

"Oh come on!" Isaac pleaded. "It's always Dr. Torre, Dr. Torre! I hate being called that! Can you just call me Isaac?!"

Captain Orvis snorted. "Very well," he said. This argument had been going on for weeks now, and he was glad to end it.

Isaac relaxed inside. Then, he refocused on the mission at hand.

"Yes, so, I have been working with the alien technology we recovered from the alien aircraft after the first of the attacks a few months ago."

He sat back down in his seat and brought up some schematics. The other three men peered at the screen.

"The technology," Isaac said glumly, "is far more advanced than anything we have here on Earth. However (he said with a smirk), I have managed to find a basic design schematic that we can use to build our own set of machines to counter the alien attack force. I've dubbed them M.A.D., after the project's codename."

Captain Orvis held up his hand. "Rylund, let's have a seat," he said. "Mr. Hall and I are familiar with the details of this project, but you will need a full briefing."

Mr. Hall gathered a few chairs from around the lab and they sat down.

Isaac continued with a nod from the Captain.

"I've made some interesting discoveries about the alien technology." Isaac said to them. He turned again to this screen and brought up more schematics. "These aliens have made technology that perpetuates using the resources about them."

"So, all the attacks on the other cities," Captain Orvis said to John, "they used the metal form the buildings...the machinery..."

"...to make more of themselves." Isaac finished. John had stayed silent.

"This technology uses a form of nanobot to create machine models like the one they came from. So, if one came from a jet, it creates more of the jet models. It need only have the resources available to do so."

John raised an eyebrow. "We don't have unlimited resources

here," he said pointedly.

"No we don't." Isaac conceded. "But, we have some, and that's how I made..."

He pulled out a device from his pocket and clicked a button on it. The wall opened up to their right, and, inside a large cavernous space, sat a jet.

The lights went on the in space, revealing a small army of other mini jets. The light in the space revealed itself for what it was: a hangar.

"Take a look, Rylund," Captain Orvis said to him.

John took a few steps forward to examine the large jet before him. The color of the jet was the standard gray, and it possessed red stripes akin to his jumpsuit. It was roughly the same size as the ones he had used in the United States Air Force, but it seemed a bit slimmer. The wing span was roughly the same. Yet, it had an indefinable quality about it that seemed...alien.

"I call it the Fire Flyer!" Isaac said proudly.

John turned and looked at him skeptically. "Fire Flyer? What kind of name is that?"

Isaac frowned. "I did design it...," he muttered.

John shook his head. *As long as it works*, he thought. He then looked around at the small mini-jets nearby.

"Well, that certainly is quite a few jets," John said. "Bit small, aren't they?"

"Yes, but they have the same firepower as the larger one." Isaac replied. "Using the alien technology, the jet engines produce not only your momentum for takeoff and flight, but the laser cannons that you can fire upon the enemy with."

"Well, I can pilot just about any aircraft or jet," John said confidently. "But, what about the other smaller jets? I'm just one man. I can't pilot all of them at once."

"I have added a neuro-helmet inside the cockpit," Isaac said. "You will be able to control the other jets with your mind. If you want maneuvers done, you can give them the instruction with the speed of thought."

A look of worry crossed John's face. "This kind of firepower could be dangerous in the wrong hands. We have had quarrels in the colony as of late. We cannot have anyone getting access to this, even by accident."

"I agree." Captain Orvis said. "We will take no chances with any of it. Maximum level security. Code 5."

He glanced at Mr. Hall, his head of security, who nodded.

"Also, I built in another security feature." Isaac said. He reached over and tapped a few keyboard buttons, and a smaller cylinder column shot up from the ground. Upon it was a small, red device, about the size of a wallet.

"This is the M.A.D. Red, or Machine Activation Device Red." Isaac said proudly. "The only one who can use the Fire Flyer is the one who possessing this M.A.D."

"Then..." John asked. "Why can't someone else use the M.A.D. Red to pilot the Fire Flyer?"

"D.N.A.," Isaac said simply. "The M.A.D. Red will only work for the first one who touches it, save for myself because I have to work on it. Once you touch it, the Fire Flyer is at your command only. No one else."

"And...what happens if I die then? Can it be given to someone else?" John asked. He looked stern and serious. The protection of the colony was the top priority in all of this.

"No," Isaac said flatly. "The D.N.A. match cannot be changed once the initial selection happens. Should you die...well, that would be it. As I said, no one else can use it."

Isaac sat solemn and silent for a few moments while they all digested his words. Things were so dire to protect the colony, it would seem mad to put such a lock in place. But, with all the fights, quarrels, and unrest that happen in the colony now, they simply could not risk this getting into the wrong hands.

"It would have been our best shot, anyway" Captain Orvis said resignedly. He turned to John. "Well, Rylund, you know the risks and what this entails."

He gestured to the M.A.D. Red.

John stepped up the platform and looked down at the device. This simple device is the last chance to save humanity. How simple things had been only a few months ago. He was living on base, awaiting assignment – when they attacked. They seemed to attack every corner of the planet at once. All the major cities of the world were destroyed. Every military base decimated. A group of people had established a hidden colony near the mountains in the west to hide from the aliens – hoping they could survive. John had traveled with what remained of his military unit to the colony.

Not all of them made it.

The colony, Terra, had indeed been a safe haven. But, the alien attacks continued on the mainland. They did eventually find the colony, and attacks started focusing there. John, having had the training in the United States Air Force to pilot aircraft, had offered to take part in this secret plan to fight back. Now, he gazed down at device, the hope of the colony, along with a sidelong look at the Fire Flyer.

He reached out and grabbed the device.

It hummed and glowed.

It beeped.

The screen flashed his name – thanks to the colony's registration files – and under his name it said: M.A.D. Red – Fire Flyer Pilot.

Chapter 2

"Well," John said. "That's that."

At that moment, sirens blared around the colony. The red lights along the corridors and hallways began to flash, and they started to hear the explosions of aircraft fire and bombs outside the colony's walls.

"THE ALIENS! THEY'RE ATTACKING AGAIN!" Captain Orvis yelled. "HALL! GET THE COLONISTS SECURED DOWN IN THE BARRACKS!"

"Yes Sir!" Mr. Hall replied. He saluted and headed off.

The Captain turned to John. "RYLUND! GET IN THE AIR!"

"Yes Sir!" John replied, saluting.

John turned to Isaac. "Alright," he said to him. "Show me how to start this up!"

Isaac nodded and he and the Captain led John to the Fire Flyer.

John, having worked with aircraft for the majority of his military career, certainly knew how to enter a jet. However, flying the machine could be a different matter altogether. If he understood that speech he had just heard correctly, the Fire Flyer was made using alien technology. While it would still follow most navigation abilities of aircraft from the planet Earth, there could still be some parts of it that were unintelligible to him.

He found the ladder and entered the cockpit. He hoisted himself inside and sat down. Once inside, he had a chance to look at the control console while he strapped himself in. He recognized many similar features of Earth aircraft – such as the various dials that showed altitude and speed. However, smack in the middle of all of them was a large viewing screen that was currently blank.

And, most unsettling, there was no flight stick.

"Rylund!" he heard Isaac yell. "Place the M.A.D. Red into the control module! That will start it!"

John lifted his head and peered out the left side towards Isaac. "THE WHAT?!" John yelled.

"There is a slot on the left for the M.A.D. Red!" Isaac yelled back. "Put it in there!"

John scanned the left side of the console quickly and found the slot that Isaac must have meant. He placed the M.A.D. Red into the slot vertically, and he watched as wires and lights came to life before his eyes. The large black screen now showed a schematic of his Fire Flyer jet as well as the smaller mini jets around him.

The glass dome of the cockpit came down over him and snapped down into position. He then heard a device above him come down and push into his head.

A helmet, he thought to himself. *At least some things don't change.*

The helmet fit snugly over his head, like it was made for him (which given his selection over a week ago it probably was). Then, just as the visor slid down over his eyes, he could feel wires and prongs poking into his head underneath the helmet.

"Uhh...," John muttered.

"Rylund!" Isaac said through some static, and John realized he was hearing a radio transceiver in his ear. "Don't worry about the wires and prongs in your helmet. They're just attached to your skull so the thoughts in your brain can be transmitted to the Fire Flyer and the small mini jets!"

"IS THIS ON?!" John heard Captain Orvis bark. After a moment more, John heard him say: "That's more like it. Now, Rylund, we are going to open the hangar door to let you fly out and engage the enemy. We're counting on you to fend off these aliens!"

No pressure, John thought.

"You can start it when you're ready!" Isaac said through the static.

And, how do you start it up?

As he thought those words, he heard the engine of the Fire Flyer fire up and blare in the hangar (thankfully, the helmet covered his ears or the sound would have deafened him). He looked on his control monitor, and he saw the lights of the mini jets light up and blare as well. Life readings showed the fire power levels and energy of the Fire Flyer and the mini jets.

He then looked forward, and he saw the door of the M.A.D. Hangar open up to reveal the blue sky of the Earth...

...and a terrifying sight.

Hundreds of the alien planes and aircraft were flying around and about the colony of Terra. They fired lasers and missiles, doing whatever they could to reach the last surviving colony of human beings.

Why? John wondered, along with the rest of the colony. *Why are they killing us off? Why did they come here?*

"ARE YOU READY, RYLUND!?"

The Captain's voice brought him back from his thoughts.

"Yes sir!" John replied.

"Then LAUNCH!"

John only had to think the order, and he felt the Fire Flyer tilt. He soon had the nose of the Fire Flyer pointing towards the exit door of the hangar. John grabbed the arm rests at his sides, and he urged the jet forward...

...and he felt his body thrown against his seat.

The speed of the jet was incredible. He had never flown in a craft that flew so fast and had such acceleration.

"WHOA!" he yelled, as he felt the Fire Flyer side swipe one of the enemy jets with its incredible speed, sending the alien craft spiraling. John felt the impact in the cockpit.

"Rylund! Take control of that thing!" Isaac yelled to him. "Keep yourself relaxed!"

John took a long deep breath as the Fire Flyer sped along. He felt it ease up slightly and he managed to bank the craft around to approach the aliens...who were coming straight at him.

"Time to test this out!" he yelled. "FIRE!"

He watched as a pair of red hot lasers fired from the sides of the Fire Flyer, blasting two of the aircraft out of the sky before him. He did a quick evade to dodge the other three that followed, narrowly avoiding their lasers blasts.

"I NEED MORE FIREPOWER THAN THIS!" John bellowed.

"It's coming!" Isaac said. "Your words just activated the smaller jets. Here they come!"

John saw it on his screen as well. The small mini jets had come to life and were flying towards him – already firing at the attacking alien force. Enemy jets fell from the sky at John's onslaught.

"Feels good to get back at these invaders, doesn't it, Isaac?!" John heard the Captain yell through the radio.

John heard the distinctive sound of a back-slap.

"Y-Yes...," John heard Isaac say through what seemed to be a cough. "Not so hard next time! John, five of the jets are coming towards you to do repairs. Don't be alarmed."

"Repairs?" John said, puzzled as he avoided another attack. "But, I'm still in combat. We can't repair the jet in the middle of all this!"

"Want to make a bet on that?"

John looked at his screen in the cockpit.

"You're joking...," he said in awe.

By the screen, John saw that he had sustained wing damage when he had crashed into the alien craft exiting the cockpit. The mini jets were actually acting as repair modules and repairing the jet while it was flying at top speeds.

"That's incredible!" Captain Orvis yelled over the radio. John was still firing on alien craft while this repair was happening. The smaller jets seemed to take no notice of his aerial maneuvers.

"It's the alien technology," Isaac replied, the static bad due to debris and combat action in the sky. "It was such an advanced code I barely understood it myself. But, this is what it does!"

"How goes the battle from your end, Rylund?" Captain Orvis asked.

"I'm holding them off, sir!" John responded. He was flying around the perimeter of the colony, looking down on the mountain and the debris of alien ships all around it. The gun turrets of the colony also fired, but that firepower was never going to keep the colony safe forever with these kind of onslaughts.

The mini jets of the Fire Flyer had been attacking in groups of 4 or 5 to a squad – under John's mental direction. It was actually quite easy. Once an order was given for tactic or strategy, the jets easily responded. They took knowledge from John's mind about how such attacks worked and responded accordingly.

"Isaac," John asked during the fight. "How many of these little jets are helping me right now?"

"We started with roughly 30." Isaac said through static. "It was all I could make with the resources I had. But so far, none have fallen in the fight. You really know your stuff!"

Soon the sky was filled with many fewer alien craft than before. John did a final circle of the colony, and he could not see no more than 15 enemy aircraft remained.

He then watched as the alien crafts began to hover close together and move away in the opposite direction.

"THEY'RE LEAVING!" Captain Orvis yelled. "YOU DID IT RYLUND!"

Isaac was cheering as well.

John breathed a sigh of relief. *At least we're all safe for now*, he thought.

Chapter 3

A few moments after the battle had ended, John heard Isaac through his helmet communicator.

"John, go ahead and bring the Fire Flyer back in!" he said. "The other jets will follow and gather together in the hangar."

John had the Fire Flyer tilt slightly to his right, and he approached the hangar door. He had to admit that this first flight had really taken him by surprise. Not only had the Fire Flyer handled beautifully, but he had an arsenal that made him a powerful air fighting force. He allowed himself a small smile.

Not everyone is this lucky, he thought.

As the Fire Flyer glided into the hangar, he could feel the engine winding down. He felt the landing gear descend and the landing into the hangar was very smooth – nothing like the jets on Earth (at least that he had flown).

He could feel the wires and probes detach from his head and the helmet lift off of him. The glass cockpit dome opened up with a gust of air.

He unstrapped himself and stretched his arms. He stood up to see Isaac and the Captain standing nearby.

"Excellent work, Rylund!" Captain Orvis yelled in triumph. "We showed those aliens whose boss!"

"Not a bad first flight," Isaac said. Then, he frowned. "But, did you have to damage the wing on takeoff?"

"I didn't mean it!" John said defensively. "I didn't think it would take off so fast! I know better now!" He then realized that he had wanted to ask something. "Isaac, how is it possible that the mini jets were able to repair the Fire Flyer while flying at full speed?"

"That's the beauty of this technology," Isaac explained. "The moment you took damage, the mini jets, seeing that the 'main ship' was damaged, flew in to make repairs. They are actually finalizing those repairs now. Look!"

John hadn't looked to the damaged wing, but when he looked, his eyes went wide. The smaller mini jets had been deconstructing themselves to form the new wing of the Fire Flyer. They were indeed still working, and John was amazed to watch the parts deconstruct and reconstruct like puzzle pieces.

"What will we do," John asked, turning back to Isaac, "about the lost mini jets? As you said, we don't have many resources."

"That's another amazing part of this technology," Isaac said smiling and pointing over towards the side of the hangar.

John looked again to watch some of the other mini jets landing...with destroyed alien ships. The jets were in the process of removing needed parts from the ships and reconstructing new mini jets for use.

"It will take them time," Isaac said. "But, they should be able to create enough mini jets, if not more, to replace the lost ones."

John stepped out of the cockpit and was climbing back down the ladder. He stepped back onto the ground and shook the Captain's hand.

"Those aliens will return, Rylund." he told him. "But we're all counting on you to keep the colony safe."

"I will," John replied.

Captain Orvis released his grip on John's hand. His face turned to a scowl, and he reached up and rubbed his forehead.

"Are you alright, Captain?" John asked him.

He gave a weak smile. "It's nothing. I've been getting these headaches lately. Must be all these alien attacks."

John nodded. "I guess I can get out of this jumpsuit now."

"Actually," Captain Orvis said. "I'd rather you wear it from now on."

"You want me to wear this all the time?" John said skeptically.

"It will let people know that you're the one who's protecting them," Isaac said. "Plus...I worked hard on it..."

"Well, I certainly don't want to dismiss your work," John said to him. He gestured to the Fire Flyer.

Isaac blushed slightly.

"We should let the colonists know the good news," Captain Orvis said. He brought his communicator out.

John nodded, but he felt a knot in his stomach. He was never that good around crowds. In his military experience, he had never gotten much praise for his actions. The hard work and dedication was praise enough – as well as the admonishment of his superiors. But, standing in front of a crowd and having praise? That was something new. He gulped.

"Alien attack has ended. Colonists may be released." he said firmly. "Gather them into the Great Chamber." The alarms and sirens had already gone off, but it was his duty to give the all clear.

"Should I keep this?" John asked, holding up the M.A.D. Red for them to see. He had taken it out of the console in the Fire Flyer.

"Yes," Isaac said. "And don't lose it! It's pretty durable, so it should not break if you drop it, but still be careful with it. I just have some small details to check here in the lab, so I'll catch up soon."

"Very well, Isaac," Captain Orvis said. "Come on, Rylund."

The Captain led the way from the M.A.D. Hangar into the main part of the Terra colony. Walking briskly, they made their way towards the Great Chamber at the very center.

"I know that jumpsuit may seem a bit silly to be wearing all the time," Captain Orvis said to John.

"We'll, I've worn them before," John admitted, as if it was necessary with his military background.

"Yes you have. In every war, there are heroes, Rylund. Images throughout history have gone with heroes and what they represent to the people. I think Isaac's design of that suit has merit."

Now that project M.A.D. had launched and was a success, Captain Orvis, though still concerned about the future, knew a chance had been born. He wanted to help raise the morale of the colonists a bit.

Several minutes later, they arrived. The entire colony was arriving from the security barracks at the lower levels and assembling there in the Great Chamber, the official meeting area of the colony. Many tables, chairs, and benches were set up here, and the large podium was up as well. This chamber also served as the dining area for the colonists (the mess hall was just off to the side).

Captain Orvis approached the podium while the rest of the colony was gathering inside. John took a chair nearby and set it up to face the assembled crowd.

"Attention, Terra citizens!" Captain Orvis' voice boomed over the speaker. The colony went quiet after a few moments. All of the colonists were gazing up front.

These people had come from all over, trying to reach this last haven for humanity. Many families with children huddled around their parents looking for some comfort. Some of the smaller children were orphaned and had been brought to the colony by people who cared and brought them to safety. All had been adopted by loving adults without question. The goal was to survive. The past was unimportant.

"As you all know, the attacks of the aliens proceed almost daily since we all gathered here at the Terra colony," Captain Orvis began. No one said anything, it was a known fact. It was only the small gun turrets and the hard shell of the colony that kept them safe from death.

"The other day, I had asked for a volunteer to help pilot a weapon that we felt would help to save and protect the colony," he said. Again, no one sound anything.

"John Rylund, the former Air Force Officer of the United State Air Force, had agreed to participate in this mission," he said, gesturing to John.

At that moment, Isaac hurried into the Great Chamber, grabbed a chair and sat it and himself down next to John.

Captain Orvis raised an eyebrow at him. Isaac gulped.

"Rylund," Captain Orvis began again, "along with our scientific adviser, Dr. Isaac Torre, were successful in fending off the enemy forces that attacked our colony."

The crowd erupted into yells and cheers. A few phrases could be heard. "Are we safe now?" "Will they be back?"

The Captain raised his hand for silence, and, after a few moments, the crowd calmed down. Security personnel led by Mr. Hall stood around the crowd in fatigues in case of any problems.

"The aliens have not been defeated. They will be back," he said simply. The crowd stood silent, awaiting the next proclamation.

"Rylund will use all the skills at his disposal to protect us as best he can," Captain Orvis continued. "Please, offer your support to him as he endeavors to protect us."

John stood up at this and approached the end of the platform. He gave a simple wave. The crowd cheered at his sight. He knew life at the colony would never be the same.

Chapter 4

John returned to his quarters exhausted from the day's activities. Not only had he been introduced to the awesome responsibility of defending the entire human colony from alien invaders, but then he had been ambushed by the adulation of the colonists from every part of the colony.

"Hey John! Great job kicking some ass out there!"

"Were they running in terror at your skills?"

"We're counting on you man!"

"Mr. Rylund, I drew this picture of you!"

That last one got him choked up. He put the picture up on the wall of his quarters with a tack.

He sat down on his easy chair. He pulled the M.A.D. Red from his pocket and stared at it.

The attention...

It's not like people did not know who he was. John had been a mainstay of the colony since it was started a few months ago. He had been working with the security force since then. Fights did break out in the colony over many issues: duty rosters, general panic, unrest, etc. So yes, people knew who John Rylund was.

He had always been a fairly quiet man, content to live his life in peace and quiet. Not that there had been many times to have peace and quiet what with the aliens attacking. But, most people tended to see him as a strong, simple, reserved man with a moderate disposition. Now, with everyone giving him this attention wherever he went...

...and this level of attention was a bit uneasy.

"Rylund!" he heard the M.A.D. Red suddenly yell out in the Captain's voice. John jumped in surprised.

"Yes sir!" John replied firmly.

"I wanted to say again, great job out there," Captain Orvis said. "I saw how people were swarming you today. You're not used to such attention are you?"

John thought a moment before replying. "No sir, I am not."

"I can certainly understand," Captain Orvis replied seriously. "You've been given a huge responsibility to defend us all. People are going to look up to that. You're giving them hope, Rylund. But, such attention can get to people."

John breathed in deeply. He knew the responsibility when he took the job. It seemed Captain Orvis, in his wisdom, seemed to know just how things had gone here in the colony.

"I can handle it," John replied, his voice firm.

"Excellent," Captain Orvis said. "I have spoken with the department heads and asked that they speak with their workers, try to lay off you a bit. You have work to do, and we cannot afford to have you distracted."

John nodded. That would make things a bit easier.

"We will inform you if, and when, the aliens return." Captain Orvis continued, back to business. "Actually, according to Isaac, the M.A.D. Red itself will. Don't understand how, but its not my job. Until then, relax. I have spoken with Mr. Hall, and a few new recruits will be taking on your duties in the security offices."

"Thank you, Captain," John replied.

"Over and out."

John tucked the M.A.D. Red back into his pocket. He was feeling hungry, but he just wanted to sit in his quarters for just a few moments more. His quarters were sparely furnished – no one in the colony could really afford to be flashy, as there was not a lot to go around. He had a table and a few chairs in his main sitting room as well as his bed, and a small shelf with some small possessions he had brought from his old life – before the aliens. They included a few books, some trinkets, and his favorite fly fishing rod. He had a small kitchenette as well as a small bathroom. Nothing special.

Suddenly, there was a knock at the door.

22

Uhh, no more today, John thought to himself.

He stood up and walked to the door, opening it.

"Dr. Cullen!" John said in surprise. "What brings you here?"

Dr. Maggie Cullen was one of the medical staff of the colony – and John was in her group of patients. She had a kind of sweet personally about her, but it did not in any way detract from her skills as a doctor. She had been handling many of the wounded individuals who had come to the Terra colony, and it took a strong will – and stomach – to be able to handle some of the gruesome injuries she tended to.

John had to admit she was fairly attractive as well. He had to guess they were roughly the same age, as he could see some flecks of gray in her short curly brown hair.

"I just came to see how you were doing," Dr. Cullen said. "That first battle must have rattled you a bit."

John looked skeptically at her. "I would have come to the medical faculty if I had suffered injury, Dr. Cullen."

"Oh, I know!" she said, her cheeks starting to blush red. "I just thought..."

"...you'd just thought you'd come and spend some time with the big hero of the colony?" he said lifting an eyebrow.

"Well...," she said nervously.

"Please come in Dr. Cullen," John said graciously.

He stepped aside, and Dr. Cullen entered into his quarters.

"Please sit down," he said, gesturing to one of the chairs.

She took a seat and John sat in the chair next to his.

"Now, why have you come here?" John asked her firmly.

"Well," she began. "I did want to check on you..."

She stopped suddenly, and her eyes narrowed as she examined John's hair.

"What is that?!" Dr. Cullen said in alarm. She reached up and brushed John's hair, pushing it aside to examine his scalp.

"How did you get these contusions?" she asked him. A series of red welts now covered his scalp.

"OUCH! EASY!" John winced. "Those are just from the combat I came from!"

Dr. Cullen looked at him, tilting her head. "Why would you have welts on your scalp and no other injuries?"

John went into a brief explanation of the prongs that had

23

entered his brain with the helmet he wore. Dr. Cullen listened intently.

"Does it look really bad?" John asked her, his voice slightly concerned.

"No, they should heal easily enough," she said soothingly. "But, I wouldn't rub your scalp too hard in the shower."

She brought her hands down from his head...and they met his hands.

John gripped her hands lightly.

Dr. Cullen blushed again, slightly embarrassed with herself. Then, she felt something cold and metal against her fingers.

Looking down, she noticed the gold wedding band on his ring finger – which she had seen during his colony physical.

"OH!" she gasped in surprise. "I'm sorry! I forgot..."

John stayed silent, his eyes downcast.

"She...," Dr. Cullen asked meekly. "She...isn't around anymore, is she?"

John nodded.

"The aliens?" she asked.

John stayed still for a moment. Then, he nodded once more.

Dr. Cullen broke her grasp with his hands. She cleared her throat.

"I just wanted to tell you how proud I am of you," she said to him. "You've accepted such a huge responsibility.

"Well, I do thank you." John said, lifting his head to meet her eyes. People had been saying that to him, but, for whatever reason, he liked hearing it from Dr. Cullen.

Especially from her lips.

"I know you've been hearing that from everyone, but I...," she seemed to hesitate, if it she wanted to say something more, but she shook her head slightly, as if stopping a thought. John watched her, admiring her brunette curls and blue eyes.

"...that I'm there at the medical facility whenever you need it," she finally said.

"Well, I surely appreciate that," John replied, smiling at her. "This will certainly be dangerous for me."

Dr. Cullen stood up. "I really should be getting back to the medical offices. I am glad that you're doing well, Mr. Rylund."

John stood up to show her out, and he took her hand. Dr.

24

Cullen stopped, and looked up into his eyes.

"Mr. Rylund, I don't want to...," Dr. Cullen began.

"Dr. Cullen," John said. "I want to tell you that I really appreciate your coming to see me. You're company makes me feel not so alone in this colony."

He leaned in and kissed her cheek.

She blushed a glorious shade of red.

"Thank you," she said. "And, please, call me Maggie."

"John," he replied.

Chapter 5

Maggie walked away from Mr. Rylund's quarters.

John's quarters, she thought.

Damn, I'm foolish! I can't be distracting him now, not when the fate of the colony rests on his ability to defend us all. Stupid, stupid!

She came to the elevators that would lead her back to the medical offices – she still had work to do. She pushed the buttons and the door closed.

As the elevator moved, she could not help but smile. In his jumpsuit, he seemed even more handsome then before. Something about the bravery he had in taking on such a responsibility had made him so charming to her...not to mention his shoulders...

Without thinking, she looked into the glossy surface of the elevator wall and checked her hair.

After a few moments, the doors slid open and she stepped out, heading towards the medical offices.

As she walked in, a man called out: "There you are, Dr. Cullen!"

Maggie turned and saw Dr. Duncan, the head of the medical department, walking towards her with a stern look on his face. A nurse followed him carrying a clipboard.

Damn it, she thought. *What is it this time?*

"Where have you been?!" he asked her accusingly, his dark eyebrows tensed.

Maggie scowled. "I was checking up on my patient, John Rylund," she told him evenly. "He just returned from his first direct fight with the aliens, and I thought I should make sure he was alright."

Dr. Duncan took the clipboard from the nurse, scanning it. "I received no instructions for his direct care," he replied. "Also, I've been given instructions from Captain Orvis that he is not to be bothered with. Anyway, I need you here in the infirmary, Dr. Cullen. I cannot have you wondering about on your own whims."

Maggie listened intently. She knew where this was heading and decided to cut him off.

"Oh," she said in mock surprise. "So, you just want me here...*with you?*" She said the last words sharply.

Dr. Duncan's face flushed. He turned to the nurse with them. "Would you please excuse us? Check up on the patient in room 5A."

The nurse hurried off. Dr. Duncan turned back to Maggie.

"Maggie," he told her quietly. "The patients need you here. I need you here..."

"Herman," she interrupted firmly. "I know patients need me here. John Rylund is one of my patients. I will not ignore one of my patients because you want me to be closer to you."

Herman took two deep breaths. "You know how much I care for you," he told her softly.

"Yes, I do," she replied. "You would do well to remember that our patients come first. Now, where do you need me, Dr. Duncan?"

Herman, seeing the discussion was closed, turned to the clipboard again. "Hmm, bed 4B has been having some seizures again. Oh, and Naomi is in your office to see you."

Maggie nodded and walked past Dr. Duncan. Herman watched her off, shaking his head sadly.

I wish he would stop this nonsense with me, she thought to herself.

A few of the on-call nurses greeted her, and she headed towards her office in the back. A few of the hospital beds were occupied by patients with terrible bloody injuries that had yet to fully heal. In 4B, a man lay in bed, groaning softly. She had gotten so used to the moaning by now. She made a note on his chart that he needed a higher dose of pain killers...

...of what we have, she thought sadly.

She arrived at her office, and the young woman there stood up to hug her.

"Hey, Maggie!" the girl said cheerfully.

"Oh, hello Naomi!" Maggie said, returning her hug.

Naomi Reins was Maggie's niece, and her only relative in the colony. Maggie had been caring for Naomi after her father, Maggie's brother, had passed away roughly 5 years ago. Naomi had never called Maggie 'aunt'. They treated each other much like sisters.

"I had some time off from work in the Agro department, and I thought I would come and see how you're doing," Naomi said, sitting back down.

Maggie sat down in the chair opposite her. "Well, the usual injured patients we've been taking care of," she said. "The load has not been as bad as it had been for some weeks, but we are still getting some colonists coming in with nervous breakdowns and panic attacks over the alien strikes."

"I don't blame them," Naomi replied, taking a deep breath. "A lot of the Agro crew is on edge as well."

They sat silent for a few moments, and then Naomi piped up: "Oh! That new herb is growing strong. We should be able to bring up some samples to test in a few days."

"Thank you for that," Maggie replied. "We are short on medical supplies, so any natural herbs you can produce would certainly be welcome."

Naomi leaned back in her chair. "What did Herman want?" she asked Maggie.

"Oh, the usual, you know," Maggie told her with a sigh. Then, mocking Herman's tone, she said: *"Come away with me, Maggie!"*

They both laughed.

"He's never going to get it, is he?" Naomi said sadly, shaking her head.

"No," Maggie replied. "But, I have to put up with him. You and I wouldn't be here if not for him."

"I know," Naomi said somberly.

Dr. Duncan had been a mutual colleague of Maggie's for years. When the aliens had attacked, Dr. Duncan contacted Maggie to tell her about the colony of Terra – that they could find refuge there – and that Maggie's skills could be of use.

She had, of course, insisted upon taking Naomi with her.

However, over the time spent there, it became clear that Dr. Duncan had a certain fondness for her – one of which she did not reciprocate.

He was a bit too...eh.

That had caused a rift between Dr. Duncan and herself that, at times, did make it difficult to work with him.

"I don't know what to do with him really," Maggie said finally. "But, we have to keep up hope that this will all work out."

Naomi's face turned to a scowl. "That's what everyone says! 'Things will work out!'" She stood up and paced back and forth in frustration. "That's how it's been since we got here!"

"Now, Naomi," Maggie said soothingly, herself still seated. "You have to look on the happier side of things. The M.A.D. project just launched, and it seems to have been a success. I mean, we are alive, aren't we? It's not as if everything has been bad."

Naomi stopped pacing and slumped herself down in the chair again. She fingered a bracelet on her wrist.

"No," she said grinning. "I guess not."

Maggie looked at the bracelet and frowned. *"You know how I feel about him."* she said sternly.

"Oh, come on, Maggie!" she protested. "I'm 19 years old! I'm not a kid anymore!"

"That boy is nothing but trouble!" Maggie told her, shaking her head. "Honestly, of all the young men in this colony, you had to choose...*him!*" she accentuated the last word.

Naomi crossed her arms indignantly. She was not going to be told at 19 years who she could and could not be dating.

Then, a sly smile crossed her face.

"So, how was Mr. Rylund?" she asked sweetly.

Maggie's face flushed at his name. "O-oh," she stammered. "He was well. I told him that the medical faculty was available if he ever needed it."

"Really?" Naomi said, pushing her face towards her aunt to tell her she was in the know.

Maggie smiled and laughed. "OK, I admit it!" she said. "I wanted to see him up close."

"OH!" Naomi said mockingly. "And was he all the man you

dreamed he was?"

"NAOMI!" Maggie scolded. "I don't want to...to...to distract him from his duties!"

"Oh yes...," Naomi said nodding. "You just want to be part of those duties..."

They both laughed. It was nice to laugh...there hadn't been that many things to laugh about lately.

"If you want it, go for it Maggie," Naomi said simply. "You cannot just work with the injured and be all duty bound all the time...that was Ricky says."

Maggie cringed at that name. "Me going after John is one thing, but Ricky..."

"OH! So, his name is *John*, it is?" Naomi countered quickly.

"Oh, give it a rest!" Maggie snapped at her.

Naomi giggled a bit then stopped. "I have to get back to the Agro department, so I will see you later, OK Maggie?" she said, rising to leave.

"Oh, I hope you don't have to work so late that you miss dinner again," Maggie said, standing along with her and giving her a hug. "Oh! And don't forget to let me know when the plants are ready!"

"I won't forget! See you later!" Naomi said with a wave and left.

Maggie walked behind her desk and looking over some of the paperwork that was left for her that day. Changes in medications, new patients arrivals, staffing changes, etc. Just the usual.

Naomi was right, as much as Maggie did not want to admit it. She did work quite a bit. Perhaps having some fun sometimes would help ease her stress...and help the gray hairs she had been getting as of late.

But, was it wise to be pursuing John, especially when he was trying to protect and save them all? She could not imagine if that was the right thing to be doing for everyone else.

But then she thought: *I'm not really doing what I'm doing for everyone else, am I?*

She looked at the time and saw that the dining area would be open soon. Perhaps she would run into him there.

Chapter 6

Naomi hurried back to the Agriculture Sector, eager to check on the herbs that they had been growing. She hoped that the sprinkler systems she had fixed were still working correctly.

Her duties in the Agro sector mostly involved maintenance. She was determined to do something to help out in the colony, and they needed maintenance workers. She had learned most of it on the fly, and so, here she was repairing broken down systems in the Agro sector.

She arrived in the Agro sector to the cheerful greeting of the mostly elderly crew. The maintaining of plants and foods was not a stressful task, so the older residents of the colony took care of the seeding, fertilizing, and reaping of the foods. Most of the food being grown had been accelerated to suit the needs of the colony population (waiting for regular growth was not an option).

Naomi checked in with the director there, and then she did a routine check on the sprinklers system she maintained.

A few hours later, she was about to start a new row when she noticed a plant near her starting to rustle. It was odd in that there was no wind or breeze in the Agro sector.

She smiled. *Really?* She thought to herself.

She continued down the row, watching the plant. It continued to rustle as she got closer.

She was finally next to the rustling plants when she decided to test the sprinklers in that set. She pressed the test button and watched as the mist flowed from the hoses she set up, covering the plants nearby.

"ARGH! NAOMI! GEEZ!" a man yelled from behind the plants.

"Gotcha!" she said.

A young man stood up from behind the plants, his short hair dripping wet and his shirt dampened. He stepped out into the aisle and Naomi giggled at him.

Ricky was a tall young man that Naomi had met in the colony a few weeks ago when they arrived. He had approached and offered to help with their bags.

Naomi had fallen for him.

Yes, her aunt was right. He had no assigned job in the colony. But, he was so cute in her eyes. He loved to party and joke, and he was always making her smile.

"You knew I was there, and you went and got me wet!?" he protested.

"I'm in the middle of my work," she said, smirking at him. "I had to test the sprinkler system."

"Yeah, you just wanted to see me all wet," Ricky said suavely.

Naomi smiled for him. He loved her smile.

She stepped down from the ladder she was on, and they embraced each other. *Damn, he's a good kisser*, she thought.

He pulled his lips from hers. "Are you free later tonight?" he asked her. "My room is gonna be awfully lonely."

Naomi looked at him. She did love spending time with him, but she couldn't get her aunt's words out of her head.

"Ricky," she said, "What did you do today?"

"Eh, just walked around," Ricky told her dismissively. "Not much to do around here."

"I know the janitorial department is looking for people," she said. "Why not ask..."

"A janitor?!" he said protested. He looked around briefly. "Things seem clean enough here, aren't they?"

"That's not the point!" she scolded him. "We're in this...mess," she said waving her hand about. "What do you plan on doing exactly?"

"I hadn't really thought about it," Ricky said simply. "We

could die soon, so I say live it up. I'm getting some of the guys together for a party next week."

A party? Naomi thought. *It would be fun, but still...*

"Damn, you're worse than Isaac!" Ricky said, leaning against a pole and crossing his arms. "That's all he says to me 'gotta have purpose.'" Ricky waved his arms in mock gestures with his statement. He rolled his eyes. "Well, I knew Isaac would feel the way he does, being the geek he is."

"That geek is trying to save us all!" Naomi snapped at him.

"Yeah, but all he ever does is have his nose on a computer screen, typing out stuff and researching." Ricky continued. "He has no fun. It's not healthy for you, I tell you."

"Besides," he said after a pause. "I thought you liked how much fun I am."

"I do," Naomi said to him gently. *Damn you Maggie, this is your fault for putting this in my head,* she thought. "But..."

"But nothing!" Ricky said, regrouping himself. "Things are going fine for me, and you don't have to worry about what I do with my time. I'll be just fine."

Naomi stared at him for several minutes. *Is this how he was always going to be?* She wondered.

"So," he said, smiling. "Are you coming to the party next week?"

Naomi sighed. "I guess," she replied. "But, you have to make me a promise."

"A promise?" he said. "What kind?"

"Promise me you'll try to find something to do with your time in a week?" she said, trying to not to sound pleading. "I mean...er...or *I won't come to your party!*" she finished.

Ricky looked taken aback. "You won't come to my party...," he said, gathering himself, "...unless I'm doing something with my time?"

Naomi nodded.

"I feel insulted," he said, turning from her. "I thought I meant more to you than that. You said you loved me regardless what I did..."

And Ricky started to walk away.

Naomi walked after him. "Ricky, wait..."

Ricky turned and caught her in his outstretched arms. "See, I knew you couldn't resist me!"

They both laughed. Naomi composed herself. She stared into his eyes.

"I'm serious though," she said.

Ricky looked into those eyes. How could he resist?

"Alright!" he said. "In one week, I promise you, I will find a job in this colony. And, in doing so, you will come to my party."

She nodded in agreement.

"Are you hungry?" he asked. "I was just about to head to dinner in the Great Chamber."

"I could use a bite to eat," she said. "But I need to finish up here. I'll join you in about 20 minutes."

"See you then, baby," Ricky said. And with a kiss on her cheek, he left.

Naomi watched him go. She loved his swagger walk. *Why had she fallen for such a man?* She thought to herself as she turned back to her sprinkler systems.

Chapter 7

The Great Chamber was full of chatter and the sounds of silverware. The gathering of the colonists was always one of the best times. Despite all of the terrible things that had transpired in the past few months or so, being together made it seem not so bad.

John had just sat down with his tray. Thanks to the communication of the Captain, people were, for the most part, leaving him be to eat. He still got the occasional wave from someone, but he was sure he would be able to eat without being distracted by praise.

He had just cut into what appeared to be potatoes when he heard a voice say: "Hey, anyone sitting here?"

He looked up. It was Maggie.

"No!" he said, his heart lifting at seeing her again so soon. "Please sit down, Dr. Cullen."

Maggie sat across from him at the table. She smiled at him.

"I'm glad you are able to get some peace from all the praise," Maggie told him. "It must be difficult."

He nodded. "Yes," he replied. "The Captain made a point of telling all the department heads to give me some space. I assume you got the same message?"

"I did," she replied, taking a sip of water. "Dr. Duncan, my superior told me. But, it didn't seem as if my visit bothered you too much."

No, it did bother me at all, he thought, smiling.

Maggie's face tensed. "What did they tell you about the alien attacks?" she asked quietly. "Do they have any idea when they will return?"

"Nothing," John said. "We don't really know. The attacks have come in waves before. Usually, they have timing to them – every other day or so – but at this point we cannot be sure. I provided the first stable resistance to them so far, so who knows how they will react to it."

"You'll have to rest at some point," Maggie noted. "They cannot expect you to be ready all the time without rest? What will we do if they never stop their assaults?"

The thought had occurred to him.

"It is what I agreed to," he eventually said.

Maggie sighed. It bothered her to think that the only defense was one man...who could get exhausted by his mission...and that she cared for him.

"HEY JOHN!" someone yelled. John and Maggie both jumped and turned to look.

Walking towards them was a young, tall, cocky looking man. He had short black hair and a smirk on his face. His jacket was open with a white shirt underneath, and he wore an old pair of Levis.

Maggie hated every part of him.

John stared at him as he approached. The man slapped him on the back.

"Hey John!" he said excitedly. "Great job kicking some ass out there!"

The young man's loud proclamation caused a few nearby individuals to shout and clap.

John blushed, but breathed and composed himself.

"I don't believe we have met," John told him evenly.

"Oh, sorry!" he said apologetically. "Ricky Plik."

He held out his hand for John, who was still seated.

John stood up from his seat. At his full height, he stood a few inches taller than Ricky. He happened to like staring down the younger man. "John Rylund," he said, grasping Ricky's hand firmly.

"Oh, I knew who you were," Ricky said. He turned to look at the others at the table.

"Oh, hey Mags!" he said cheerfully, waving with his free hand.

"THAT'S DR. CULLEN TO YOU!" she snapped at him.

"Hey, no need to be rude, just saying hi!" Ricky said.

"You know this man?" John asked, turning to her.

"Yes...regrettably," she said frowning.

"I haven't seen you working anywhere," John said questioningly. "What department of the colony do you work for?"

"Well," he said. "I haven't found anything yet. But, I plan to in the next week or so."

"Or so...," John said in disbelief.

Ricky had averted his eyes from John's piercing glare. He turned his head and then...

"Naomi!" he yelled, breaking his handshake with John. Naomi ran over and jumped into his arms.

"I missed you!" he told her.

"I told you I'd only be a few minutes!" Naomi replied, whipping her hair out of her face.

Naomi saw her aunt. "Oh, hi Maggie!" she said cheerfully.

Maggie nodded, though a frown was on her face. "John," Maggie said, trying to remain calm. "This is my niece, Naomi."

Naomi saw the scowl on her aunt's face. "Oh don't be like that!" Naomi said. "So, this is *John*, is it?"

"John Rylund," John said, holding out his hand for Naomi. She took it and shook cheerfully.

Her eyes scanned John up and down. She winked at her aunt.

She turned back to Ricky. "Let's grab something to eat, Ricky. Come on!"

Ricky plodded after her.

"So, that's your niece?" John asked Maggie. She nodded.

"I see why you don't like him," John said to flatly, his face a scowl.

Maggie nodded, her frown tightening.

John and Maggie tucked into eat, the interruption of Ricky and Naomi having ruined the mood between them.

A few moments later, Ricky and Naomi had returned and sat down next to them. Ricky next to John and Naomi next to Maggie.

John was the first to speak.

"So," John asked Ricky, "what kind of skills do you have exactly?"

"What?" Ricky said, his mouth full of potatoes.

"Skills...abilities," John clarified. "What exactly can you do that would be of use to those here at the colony?"

Ricky swallowed. *What skills do I have?* He thought to himself.

"Well, err...," he said, thinking hard. "I like...music..."

"I didn't ask what you liked," John said sternly. "I asked what skills you have and what you can do for the colony. We're all in this together, you know."

"That's right!" Maggie snapped at Ricky. "Do something, you bum!"

"MAGGIE!" Naomi protested.

"It's the truth, Naomi!" Maggie told her fiercely, staring her down. Naomi cowered under her aunt's glare.

She turned back to face Ricky, her voice full of fury. "WHEN ARE YOU GONNA GET OFF YOUR ASS AND DO SOMETHING TO HELP OUT AROUND HERE!?"

Ricky's face was chalk white. He couldn't find his voice.

"WHOA, WHOA! What's going on?" a new voice said.

They all turned and saw Isaac walking to them, carrying his tray. His white lab coat was open, and he had spiked up his blond hair (as was his style).

Upon seeing a potential ally, Ricky finally found his voice.

"They're ganging up on me!" he said.

Both John and Maggie now glared at Ricky. Naomi looked stricken.

Isaac sat down next to Ricky. "What are you ganging up on him about?"

"THAT HE'S A WORTHLESS, NO GOOD..." Maggie started shouting, but John held up his hand and indicated nearby.

Some of the nearby colonists and families had noticed her outburst...some had small children.

Maggie breathed some deep breaths and calmed herself down.

Isaac nodded. He turned to Ricky, "Still haven't found a job yet, huh, Ricky?" he said simply.

Ricky's face flushed red. He flipped his tray in anger – mashed potatoes flying everywhere.

"I'M OUTTA HERE!" he yelled. "I DON'T HAVE TO TAKE THIS SHIT!"

He stood up and stormed off from the table.

"RICKY!" Naomi yelled. She stood up and ran after him.

"Kids," John said. He surveyed the table, noting how the potatoes had splashed everywhere. Bits of them hung from Isaac, Maggie, and himself.

Maggie had calmed, but she was still stewing.

"God, why him!?" she said, looking upward.

Suddenly, the M.A.D. Red in John's pocket blared. A communicator in Isaac's pocket went off as well.

"The Aliens!" Isaac said hurriedly, looking at his communicator. "They're attacking again! It's another air assault!"

As soon as he said it, the alarms blared throughout the Great Chamber. The security personnel stationed around the perimeter began to usher the colonists down into the security barracks as before. Some of them looked to John as they walked out.

"GO!" John bellowed to them as he stood up. "Follow security. Get to safety! GO!"

Some of them smiled and waved encouragement to him.

He breathed deep. *No pressure*, he thought.

"RYLUND!" Captain Orvis' voice sounded over the M.A.D. Red. "Report to the M.A.D. Hangar!"

John held the M.A.D. Red up to his face. "Roger that!" he replied.

John turned to Maggie, gave her a curt nod, and he followed Isaac to the M.A.D. Hangar while Maggie headed off.

Chapter 8

Ricky walked briskly from the Great Chamber. People ran the other way around him – heading for the security barracks. The alarms went off all around the hallways and red lights flashed. While it would be safer to head down, as most people did, it was not necessary.

Naomi was dodging around people quickly to catch up. She finally got past the last of the crowd.

"Ricky, will you just listen to me!" Naomi pleaded.

Ricky didn't answer. He continued towards his quarters.

Naomi caught up to him, and she grabbed his shoulder.

"RICKY!" she said.

Ricky turned around, glaring at her, with a scowl on his face.

"IS THAT WHAT YOU THINK TOO!?" he yelled. "THAT I'M JUST A BUM?!"

"NO!" she yelled back to him, a look of hurt on her face.

"That's what you said to me in the Agro Center!" he told her. "You were all about what I did with my time!"

Naomi's eyes welled with tears. Ricky, seeing her cry, started backing down.

"Hey," he said softly, putting his hands around her face. "I'm sorry..."

Naomi slapped his hands away. She was sobbing. She covered her face and ran from him down the hall.

Damn it. Ricky thought to himself.

He finally reached his quarters and walked inside, closing the door. Closing the door did cut off the alarms in the hallway, but a small alarm was buzzing on the inside wall. Ricky reached up and disconnected a wire – stopping the sound.

His place wasn't at all big: a simple living area and a bathroom off to the side. He slumped himself down in a chair and looked about, trying to calm himself. He eyes glazed over what possessions he had: his old guitar, an old CD/stereo player with a few discs, and his clothes here and there.

He was still in a bad mood. *So what if he didn't have a job? So what if he just wanted to have some fun?*

Just what his dad thought too...

He shook his head and refocused. Something else bothered him...

Naomi...Damn it! I can't believe I made her cry!

She had been the only thing that made his world shine during this whole mess, and now look what he had done!

He heard a knock on his door.

Naomi! He thought, his spirits rising. *I'll be able to mend things up in no time!*

He went to his door and opened it.

"Hey Naomi..."

POW!

"OWWW!" he yelped as he staggered back. Naomi withdrew her fist and followed in after him, shutting the door.

"Don't you EVER yell at me like that again, fucker!" Naomi told him fiercely.

"Geez!" Ricky moaned, rubbing the side of his face, a red welt showing where he got struck. "I may never yell again, period!"

Ricky backed up and sat on his couch, Naomi helping him to get seated.

"It is your own fault, you know," she told him.

Ricky said nothing as he rubbed his cheek.

Naomi pulled his hand away, examining his face.

"I got you pretty good, didn't I?" she said. She brought her hand up and caressed the bruise.

"Ah!" he moaned.

She walked to the small fridge in the room and grabbed the ice pack there. She came back and pressed it against his face.

"Ahh..." he sighed in relief, feeling the cold against his cheek. He brought his hand up to hold it in place.

They sat silent for a few minutes.

Ricky was the first to speak.

"I'm sorry," he said to her.

"I know you are," she said knowingly. "But, why do you get like that whenever anyone wants you to get off your butt and do something?"

Ricky hesitated. He wasn't sure if he knew how to answer.

"I mean...come on, Ricky!" she pressed. "You've been here three months, and all you ever do is lay about while most everyone else is trying to stay active."

Ricky still didn't answer.

"FINE, BE THAT WAY!" she said angrily, as she stood up. "I'm not going to be with a guy who just won't get off his ass!"

She made her way to the door. She had just turned the handle when she heard something behind her.

Ricky was looking intently after her, and cradled in his arms, was his guitar.

He was strumming a simple tune that she had heard many times. It was a tune he always played when she was there.

He had made it just for her.

"Ricky," she said, not moved in the slightest. "A song is not going to change my mind."

"But maybe this will," he said. He stop playing, and he got up and took her hands into his.

"When I make a promise, I keep it," he told her firmly. "When have I ever lied to you?"

He never did. She liked that about him.

"I will have a job in this colony in the week," he said firmly. "I promise."

Naomi stared at him. She hadn't heard this voice often. Perhaps the punch made its point.

But, she did believe him. She nodded.

"Now, you mind staying for a while?" he said to her. "I have this bruise on my face, and I need someone to look after me."

She laughed and sat back down on the couch next to him. She pressed the ice pack up to his face while he strummed his guitar lightly. The tune was very calming.

"Where did you ever learn to play like that?" she asked him.

"My dad. He was a guitar player," he said.

Then, he added somberly: "...this was his."

"Oh!" she said in surprise. "I never knew." Naomi's hands clasped the locket around her neck.

"You never asked," he said to her, continuing the tune he played.

Naomi put the ice pack down and laid against Ricky. He continued strumming his tune while she rested against him.

That's more like it. Ricky thought to himself. Oh, he hadn't been lying to Naomi before. He was serious about his promises. But, he felt better knowing that she still cared for him. It was nice to have someone who cared.

She must have laid next to him for at least an hour or so. The sounds of the alarms in the hallway finally stopped.

Naomi crawled herself up to his face, and she planted a kiss on his bruised cheek.

He turned and his lips met hers. He sat his guitar down as they embraced, his fingers running through her hair.

Chapter 9

An announcement came over the loudspeaker. MEDICAL TEAM TO THE M.A.D. HANGAR.

Within minutes, the on-call medical team led by Dr. Maggie Cullen had arrived at the M.A.D. Hangar of the Fire Flyer. They walked into a tense scene. Isaac and Captain Orvis were helping John out of the Fire Flyer cockpit.

John was bleeding heavily from a wound on his head.

"OH MY...WHAT HAPPENED?!" Maggie yelled as the group examined the scene.

"John got shot by one of the alien ships just as he was coming back in," Captain Orvis said.

"It was a cheap shot...," John said, his voice strained. He struggled to stay upright.

"The gurney!" Maggie said to her medics. The nurses quickly setup the gurney right there in the hangar. John was laid down on it.

Maggie was handed some towels. She began to wipe down his head.

"It looks a lot worse than it is," she explained. "The head always bleeds a lot more than other parts of the body."

Maggie finally did find the wound. A long cut across his forehead.

"It looks like a glass cut," she said, examining it.

"The dome of the cockpit shattered," Isaac said to her, pointed to the Fire Flyer's cockpit and the visible shatter. "John's lucky he didn't lose an eye."

Maggie was speaking quickly to her medical staff, asking for a suture kit and cloth for a wrap. The nurses nodded and went to work.

Maggie was applying an antibacterial wash to the wound. John winced as his wound was cleaned.

"I'll need to do stitching so it will heal properly," she said calmly to John.

John nodded slowly.

"Thank you." she said to her medical staff as the supplies were brought to her. Isaac and the Captain stood back while she did her work.

"Knows her stuff, doesn't she?" Captain Orvis remarked, watching.

"He's in good hands," Isaac said confidently.

The whole matter took only about 20 minutes to resolve. Maggie never skipped a beat on her patient, making sure that the stitching was solid and that John was kept comfortable. He was given a mild pain killer so he would be in a relaxed state.

Finally, Maggie was finished. John's face looked better. His head lay still on the pillow, breathing calmly. He was soon asleep.

"That's all I can do for now, but he needs to rest." she explained to the Captain Orvis.

He nodded.

She turned to her medics: "Bring him to his quarters." she told them, and they pushed the gurney with John out of the hangar.

"The alien ships have flown away for the moment," Captain Orvis said after John as gone. "Thankfully, Rylund was able to defend us again."

"It was a cheap trick on their part!" Isaac said, flustered. "I can't..."

A beeper suddenly went off in his pocket.

Isaac grabbed the communicator on his pocket and pushed some buttons on the screen.

"What is it?" Maggie said. She hadn't left the hangar yet.

"It's the aliens," Isaac said, heading over the computer stations. "They're attacking again!"

"DAMN!" the Captain said. "And John is out for now! What will we..."

"It wouldn't matter if John could defend us," Isaac interrupted. "It's not an air assault this time."

"It's not?" Captain Orvis said curiously.

"It's...an attack by the ocean!"

The colony of Terra was built alongside the ocean. It was this water that provided power via a hydro-electric plant, as well as the filtered drinking water for the colonists.

Isaac stared at his screen. He had switched to a sonar view. A bar turned around the screen clockwise and blips showed up on the screen heading towards the central point – the colony of Terra.

"They must be heading towards the hydro-electric plant in the hopes of destroying it to kill us off, since the air attacks have not been successful."

Captain Orvis had a hard look on his face. He was a bit nervous about his next question.

"Isaac," he said, keeping his voice steady, "did you have any plan if this kind of attack happened?"

Isaac turned and gave the Captain a sly smile. He turned back to his screen and pressed a few buttons. A schematic of a large submarine came into view.

"Behold the Aqua Marine!" he declared. "I had a launch bay built near the hydro plant for just this occasion. It runs on the same kind of technology as the Fire Flyer, but of course, it's used for nautical combat. It's sitting there waiting for use whenever we need it."

Captain Orvis smiled. It was good to have a genius who thought of things when you needed them most.

"We do need a pilot though," Isaac pointed out.

Captain Orvis tensed. "We don't really have the time..."

"I will," Maggie said from behind them.

The Captain and Isaac both jumped at her words. They had forgotten she was there, but she had been listening intently.

Maggie had been pretty frightened when the medical team had been called to the M.A.D. Hangar. She had only assumed the worse, and she steeled herself for dealing with what she thought was the inevitably --- that John had been killed. She was very level-headed when dealing with injuries at the colony.

But with John, something was different.

She cared about him...a lot, she realized.

The thought that John was at risk to this kind of injury made her nervous. If John failed, the whole colony could die, and there was nothing she could do about it. All the wounded would need help...more help then she would ever be able to give on her own. The thought of that many people being injured...being killed...and John...

Then, upon hearing about the attack via the ocean and the Aqua Marine, her mind was set on the one course of action that she could, no, *must* take.

"Dr. Cullen," Captain Orvis began, "you understand this is extremely dangerous. I wouldn't want someone inexperienced in aquatic navigation to..."

"Isaac," she said, interrupting the Captain, "That sonar shows a 3 mile nautical radius, doesn't it?"

Isaac startled. *She has been paying attention.* "Uh...yes," he replied.

"And this Aqua Marine, it can go to down to the ocean floor for reconnaissance, I assume?" she continued.

Isaac nodded. "1000 fathoms at most. That more than covers the depth needed to protect the structure of the colony beneath the water's surface."

"How is it you know such things?" Captain Orvis asked her.

"I have been scuba diving all my life, Captain," she told him, staring at him in the eye. "My father was a naval captain. You might say such things run in my family."

Captain Orvis was impressed. But, he was still concerned.

"You are a medical staff member," he reminded her. "We still have sick and wounded that need your attention."

"We have nurses and other staff that could do that," Maggie countered. "Besides, if we don't stop them (she indicated the screen), there will be more injuries and deaths here. Wouldn't you agree?"

Captain Orvis did. He nodded.

"Very well," he said. "Isaac, lead the way to Aqua Marine."

Chapter 10

And so, the colony came under assault once more, and again, a noble warrior was needed to stand against the invading aliens.

This time, a female warrior would take the helm. She would need her cunning, wit, and skill to save humanity from...

"Isaac? Is something wrong?" Captain Orvis asked him in concern.

Isaac shook his head to clear his thoughts. "Oh...sorry about that," he said. He pointed down the hallway. "This way!"

Captain Orvis had called for everyone to return to the security barracks for their protection. People were moving past them as Isaac led Maggie and Captain Orvis briskly towards their destination.

"I assume you must have this submarine bay some distance from the hydro-electric plant?" the Captain asked Isaac as the elevator went down.

"The M.A.D. Bay where the Aqua Marine is stored is only a stone throw from the plant," Isaac said. "We'll get there soon."

Alarms went off in the hallways around them and red lights flashed.

"We'd best be quick about it!" Captain Orvis said hurriedly.

Maggie breathed deeply, steeling her nerves. While she was skilled in nautical terms from her father, she certainly hadn't had experience piloting a submarine. If she understood how John's Fire

Flyer system worked, she could only assume the Aqua Marine must use a similar neural system. She hoped she could make it all work.

"Here we are," Isaac said, stopping at a doorway.

Isaac pressed some buttons on a door and pressed his hand to a panel. The door slid open, and they beheld a large launch bay. Sounds of water droplets echoed in the dimly lit chamber, and a slosh of water could be heard against a large submarine in a water pool before them.

Isaac reached to the side and flicked a switch. A few lines of lights came on above the bay, and the Aqua Marine came into view. As with the Fire Flyer, the design of the Aqua Marine was similar to ones on the planet earth, but it had that strange alien quality to it that was indefinable. It currently was floating silently in the launch bay.

"And the other mini-subs?" Captain Orvis asked.

"They are storing themselves underneath the surface," Isaac said. "Are you ready, Maggie? I can give you a primer."

He stepped over to a control station in the launch bay. Maggie and the Captain followed while Isaac brought up some schematics.

"The Aqua Marine, if it is not obvious, is a submarine," Isaac said.

"*Really?*" Maggie said in mock surprise. "I had no idea!"
She frowned at him.

Isaac chuckled. "OK, I'll skip the basics."

"It will take my orders from my thoughts, just like John's Fire Flyer?" Maggie asked Isaac.

"*John?*" Captain Orvis asked her, raising an eyebrow.

"OH!" she said, catching herself. "I mean Mr. Rylund, of course."

Isaac nodded. "In the Fire Flyer," he said, "Rylund controlled the mini jets using a neural helmet. The Aqua Marine also has a neural helmet that you will send orders to the other mini subs."

"What kind of fire power does it have?" Maggie asked him.

"Pressure torpedoes," Isaac said. "I'm afraid that's the extent of it. But, the technology uses the water itself to create missile-like force to fire upon opponents. It has pressure strong enough to crack through steel. Also, it creates air via the water around it for the user's needs."

"Well, let's get you in there," Captain Orvis said. "What's the enemy's E.T.A.?"

Isaac checked his screens. "They will be within range within 30 minutes."

Isaac pointed to a small table nearby. On it, lay a device similar to John's M.A.D. Red...

...but this one was blue.

"There it is," Isaac said to her. "Are you..."

But she had already grabbed it. The lights on the M.A.D. came on. On the front display, her name was shown, along with the words M.A.D. Blue- Aqua Marine Pilot.

Isaac led Maggie to the Aqua Marine. He walked her along the dock, and she reached over to the entrance hatch, turning the wheel.

Isaac let her continue. *She knows what she's doing*, he thought.

She flipped the hatch open and let herself inside. Dropping down, she found the space was actually quite small. There were emergency oxygen tanks, a life jacket, and the main control console. She put on the life jacket and sat down at the control console. Looking out the glass shield in front of her, she could see the dark blackness of the ocean.

"Sit down and put the M.A.D. Blue into the slot on the console." she heard Isaac say to her.

Maggie sat down in the chair and pushed the M.A.D. Blue into the slot. The console came to life.

"OK, Mag...I mean Dr. Cullen," Isaac corrected. "Pull the helmet on. The wires will attach to your head."

Maggie looked up and saw the helmet. It was one of those glass dome types that marine divers used. She pulled it down and she felt some pressure seal around neck. She breathed deeply, feeling the fresh oxygen being circulated into the helm.

Then, she felt the wires. It felt like prongs entering her curls, and she couldn't help but wince a bit as it attached.

OK, she thought. *Here we go.*

The Aqua Marine came to life at her thought. The console glowed and showed radar in front of her. Lights came on in front, and she estimated that she could see a few hundred feet in front of her.

That's not exactly perfect, she thought.

The radar spun around in it's circle, and she saw a terrifying sight. Roughly a hundred subs were heading towards her and the colony.

...and they seemed a lot closer then when she saw them before.

"We've got company," Maggie responded. "Where are the mini subs?"

In response, she saw a set of blips on the console near her position. She saw one of the subs float in front of her. It looked like a smaller version of the Aqua Marine.

"Dr. Cullen," she heard Captain Orvis say through an earpiece. "Don't you think you should..."

"Oh, right!" Maggie replied. "Let's move!"

She felt a shift in the Aqua Marine as it was released from its clamps and began to submerge into the water.

Maggie urged the Aqua Marine forward and towards the approaching blips on her screen.

She took a deep breath. *I can do this*, she said to herself.

Chapter 11

The blips on the screen approached the Aqua Marine far faster than Maggie would have liked.

Wish I had a shield, she thought to herself.

She watched on the sonar screen as the mini subs (some she saw through the glass) floated up in front of her to protect the front of the Aqua Marine.

Well, that makes me feel better. She thought.

She heard a sound in the distance. It sounded like a huge gush of water.

She saw it on the radar: a projectile was heading towards her...fast.

Can I shoot that thing? was her first thought.

On the screen, she saw one of the mini subs open fire at the projectile, she saw and heard the explosion impact in front of her...the ocean lit up for just a moment when it happened.

"Wow," Isaac said through the radio. "Nice shot, Dr. Cullen."

Then she saw many more of the enemy subs firing upon her and her subs.

"Just let the subs know to intercept that fire, Dr. Cullen," Isaac told her through static.

Maggie relayed the thought the best she could. She watched in a slight awe as the mini subs attacked and intercepted many of the projectile fire coming towards her. She marveled at the flashes of light in the ocean. It reminded her of fireworks.

Then, she watched as one of the projectiles was missed by the mini subs and came straight towards her.

She felt her stomach tighten in a knot.

"FIRE!" she shouted out loud in a fit of terror.

She felt the Aqua Marine recoil as the pressure torpedo fired. The perfect trajectory of the torpedo crashed into the incoming projectile. The explosion happened only a few hundred feet in front of her, and the force rocked the Aqua Marine and sent some of the mini subs keeling.

"Dr. Cullen! DR. CULLEN!" Captain Orvis shouted upon hearing her panic. "Are you alright!?"

Maggie recovered at his voice. "Y-y-yes...," she stammered, breathing heavy. "I'm fine! Close call! Let me get the subs back in position!"

As she said the words, the subs floated back quickly, continuing to intercept enemy fire.

Let's not let that happen again, she thought, trying to force that thought in her mind towards the subs – which she knew it was not necessary, but damn it, it made her feel better.

Shots continued firing upon her subs, and the subs managed to maintain the defense.

"Dr. Cullen, don't you think it is time for some offense?" Captain Orvis chimed in.

Maggie had been concentrating so hard on defense that she had forgotten she could fight back. "Oh, right!" she said.

She guided the mini subs and the Aqua Marine forward towards the attacking alien subs, carefully maintaining the defensive shield she had around herself.

Attacks still bombarded her, and she had to stop a few of them with the Aqua Marine's pressure torpedoes. Her mind was tense from the effort it took.

Is it this hard for John? She wondered.

When she had advanced far enough with the Aqua Marine, she could see the alien subs. Sleek and simple, they floated in the water in front of her like a swarm of bugs.

She began to fire towards the enemy. She watched through the glass as her torpedoes soared to the enemy forces. She saw explosions in the water as many of the shots hit their targets, parts of the enemy subs floated motionless in the water.

The battle continued for several tense minutes as Maggie watched the explosions in the water. A few more attacks did come towards her, and, as time continued, she started to gather the rhythm of the enemy assaults. She never relaxed during the fight, but she was able to predict (to some degree) when the attacks would come.

Finally, after what felt like an eternity (though it was roughly about a half hour or so), she finally had destroyed all the enemy subs. She breathed a sigh of relief as the radar showed no more active subs in the water. The mini-subs under her control swarmed towards the destroyed subs and began to gather up the parts. Maggie looked on in wonder.

"They are just gathering up some parts as they are programmed to do," Isaac said to her through the radio. "You did lose quite a few subs in that fight, so they are gathering spare parts to make repairs. No damage to the Aqua Marine at all. Great job, Dr. Cullen!"

Maggie breathed heavy. "Thank you," she said.

"Bring it back to the bay, Dr. Cullen," Captain Orvis said.

Maggie guided the Aqua Marine back to the bay. She took off the helmet and stood up. She was surprised to find that she was shaking. She grabbed the M.A.D. Blue and headed towards the hatch.

Opening it up, she climbed out. Her body was still shaking.

To her surprise, she found Dr. Duncan their waiting. He helped her out of the sub.

"Dr. Duncan!?" Maggie said in surprise. "What are you doing here?"

"This was your on-call shift," Dr. Duncan said quickly, "I knew you got called to the M.A.D. Hangar for an emergency. After the second all-clear, I went looking for you, and I couldn't find you in the medical office. I questioned the medical staff who worked with you, and they said you didn't leave with them. So, I contacted Captain Orvis..."

"...and I told him you were here," Captain Orvis finished.

Captain Orvis stepped onto the dock. "He is your supervisor, after all. Are you all right, Dr. Cullen?" he asked her, his voice full of concern.

"I—I'm fine," she said, trying to make her voice firm.

"You're shaking, Maggie!" Dr. Duncan said in alarm, as he walked her off the dock. "Do you need to go to the infirmary?"

"Can I just sit down?" she said to him, looking for a chair.

Isaac had brought a chair over and let Maggie sit down. She was breathing heavy, trying to control herself.

"Dr. Cullen," Captain Orvis said. "Are you going to be able to handle this?"

"Of course she can't!" Dr. Duncan shouted out, his voice echoing against the walls of the M.A.D. Bay.

Maggie glared at Dr. Duncan. She stood up slowly, her eyes staring daggers at him.

"I'll be just fine, *Herman*," she said, emphasizing the last word. She was still staring Dr. Duncan down.

Dr. Duncan's face turned to a scowl. He hated when Maggie did that with his name.

Captain Orvis had watched the exchange quietly. "I think Dr. Cullen made her choice, Dr. Duncan," he said.

Dr. Duncan turned to him. "And, what of her medical duties?" he asked him. "She can't perform her duties *and* protect the colony!"

"I will still perform some duties when I can," Maggie said firmly.

"And you have other medical staff," Captain Orvis added. "You will have to adjust your scheduling to accommodate this."

Dr. Duncan breathed heavily for several moments.

"Fine," he finally said. And he strode out of the M.A.D. Bay.

Captain Orvis turned to Isaac. "All the subs have re-docked?"

"Yes," Isaac replied. "No new enemy craft have approached that I can see. Dr. Cullen was completely successful."

"I will gather the colonists and tell them of your appointment, Dr. Cullen," Captain Orvis said. "Excellent work, again."

Captain Orvis walked out of the bay. Isaac turned to Maggie.

"Maggie," he said, concern in his voice. "I can tell you're upset. You've never been in a fight have you?"

Maggie nodded. "It was...frightening," she said in a controlled voice.

"I can bet," he said, pulling a chair alongside hers. He held some gray clothing in his hands.

"Here is the gray jumpsuit I made for the Aqua Marine's

pilot." he said, handing it to her. "It's a gray jumpsuit just like..."

"...like John's," she said, her voice weak.

"Yep, save this one has blue stripes on the sides," Isaac noted.

"You were great out there, you know?" he added, grinning. "I cannot imagine having to fight all those aliens coming at me. All the shots flying at me..."

Maggie held up her hand to stop him. She had started shaking again.

"Oh...sorry," he said, frowning. "I get carried away when I talk."

Maggie lowered her hand down and nodded, still breathing heavy.

"Hey, I have a great idea!" he said. Great ideas were his specialty. "Why not go and see how John is doing? He has to go through this himself, being in the M.A.D. as well. And, he's been in combat before that. Maybe he can offer some advice and...."

Isaac hesitated, and then added: "...some comfort?"

Maggie looked at him. She nodded once and stood up, walking to the bay exit.

Maggie stopped and turned to him, "Thank you, Isaac." she said. She then walked out the door and left.

Isaac had a feeling about John and Maggie. His hunches were usually right.

Maggie walked briskly towards John's quarters. John was exactly who she wanted to see right now.

Chapter 12

John opened his eyes. He was lying on his bed inside his
quarters.

His head was aching. He glanced at the wall clock. It was
evening.

He reached up and touched his forehead, feeling the
wrapping.

That's right, he thought. He remembered the fight he was in
with the aliens. He had managed to guard the colony again. It had
been a battle just as fierce as before, with many of his mini jets being
blown out of the sky. It was only due to his knowledge of flight
maneuvers that he was able to survive himself.

He was guiding the Fire Flyer back into the hangar when a
missile had impacted him. All he could remember was the gust of air
and glass in his eyes. He must have still been conscious, since he did
remember being pulled from the Fire Flyer while inside the hangar.

That was a close one, he thought.

John sat himself up. He felt a bit dizzy at first, but he planted
both feet on the ground. He finally stood up and walked over to his
bathroom and looked in the mirror. He washed the dried blood from
his face, and he pulled the wrapping from his forehead.

"Ouch, that one hurt," he said as he felt along the cut. The
stitching was done quite well.

Suddenly, he heard a knock on his door. He put his wrapping
back in place.

"Coming," he said. *I wonder if it's the Captain?*

He opened the door in surprise.

"Maggie!" he said, alarmed at her posture. Something was wrong.

Then he saw something else that shocked him – she's wearing a jumpsuit like his.

"Y-You're...," he stammered.

"Yes," she said weakly. Then, she started to sob.

He brought her inside and shut the door. He brought her to the bed and sat her down.

"Can I get you a glass of water?" he said, staring at her in concern.

She nodded, still sobbing.

He got the glass of water and brought it to her. He sat down on the bed next to her.

She took a long sip and sat the glass down.

"John...it was so scary...," she said. "All that...darkness..."

"Darkness?" he asked, puzzled.

Maggie then explained to him what had happened after she came to M.A.D. Hangar to assist him – how she had tended to his wounds, how the aliens had attacked again from the ocean, and how she had made the decision to help fight the aliens using the Aqua Marine.

She showed John her M.A.D. Blue.

Maggie was still sniffing, but she finally looked up at John's wound. "Let me look at that again," she said, trying to find something else to focus her mind on.

John nodded. Maggie pulled the wrapping off. "It looks like the stitching is holding," she said, looking through her bloodshot eyes. She put the wrapping back in place.

"How do you do it, John?" she said, sniffing. "How do you deal with the stress of it all?"

John sat back. *How did he handle it?*

"Well, Maggie," he began. "You make a decision to fight with all you have. You defend those who cannot defend themselves. That's what keeps you going. All that attention I received? It can be a distraction...but, it does remind me of why I do what I do."

"They were coming at me so fast, John!" Maggie said, terror in her voice. "I've never been so frightened!"

He put his hand on hers to calm her. "Yes, it is frightening, Maggie," he told her in a calm voice. "But, you did manage to pull yourself through. Didn't you?"

Maggie looked him. "I don't think I have the courage for this."

"You have more courage than you know, Maggie." he said. He leaned in and kissed her on the lips.

He broke off the kiss after a moment. "I can go over some combat tactics with you." he said firmly. "I will help you through this. I promise you."

Maggie smiled meekly.

John had put his arm around her. On impulse, he brought his lips to hers again. She kissed him back. John brought both of his arms around hers and brought her close.

"We'll get through this together," he said to her quietly.

She enjoyed his embrace. His arms made her feel safe.

John breathed heavy and unzipped his jacket, pulling it off.

This would make things complicated, they both knew. But, to be fair, things were quite complicated already.

***

Ricky woke up. His arms were around Naomi.

They were lying underneath the blankets of his bed.

He looked at Naomi. Her face was so peaceful.

Damn, she's beautiful. He thought to himself.

They had fallen asleep a few hours ago. He glanced at the clock. It was time for breakfast.

He got himself up and grabbed some clothes. He pulled his pants on.

"You have a really nice butt," he heard from behind him.

Ricky looked behind him and saw Naomi staring at him. He shook his hips for her. She giggled.

Naomi pulled herself out of bed, stretching her arms up. She got up and began to get dressed along with Ricky.

"It's time for breakfast," Ricky said. "Care to join me?"

Naomi glanced at the clock. "I have an hour before I have to be at work," she said, pulling her blouse on. Ricky noticed her grab her locket from the dresser and put it around her neck.

Come to think of it, he had always seen her wearing it. He remembered the locket from when he met her.

"What's the deal with that anyway?" Ricky asked her. He had never bothered to ask before.

Naomi hesitated. She looked Ricky in the eyes. She decided she could tell him.

She took a seat back on the bed, and she beckoned Ricky to sit next to her.

"This is the locket my dad gave me," Naomi began, as Ricky sat down. She opened the locket to reveal a picture. It showed her as a young girl. Standing next to her was a man who Ricky could only assume was her father.

"This is picture of us at a carnival," she explained. "It...was actually one of the last times I remember spending time with him. He actually bought me this locket at that carnival, and they gave you a picture to put in it...."

Naomi went silent. Ricky saw a tear in her eye. He wiped it away for her.

"Thanks," she said. "Just shortly after we got home from that trip, maybe a day or so, dad started having spasms..."

Naomi started sniffling. Tears started flowing from her eyes. She wiped them away.

"He was taken to the emergency room...," she said, trying to hold tears back. "And...he died."

Naomi was crying in earnest now. Ricky put his hand around her to comfort her.

"I-It all just h-happened...," she said, sobbing. "Maggie was there for me – she lived down the street. She said I could come live with her – she never thought twice about it, she said."

She held the locket in her hands.

"This is all I really have to remember him by now." she said, turning to look at Ricky.

"You remind me a lot of how fun he was, Ricky," she said.

Ricky smiled. "Well, I do enjoy having a good time." he remarked.

She hugged him, and he hugged back.

Naomi broke the hug from him, and looked at him quizzically. "I just realized I've never asked you about your family. What were they like?"

Ricky went silent. He moves his lips like he was going to say something, but nothing came out.

"Oh," Naomi said, "I didn't mean to remind you of...I mean they must be..."

"Forget it...," Ricky said, shaking his head. "It's alright. We have each other now, right?"

Naomi nodded, putting the locket around her neck.

"Come on," Ricky said, standing up. "It's time for breakfast!"

And Ricky walked Naomi out of his quarters and towards the Great Chamber.

Chapter 13

John woke up under his bed covers, his arms around Maggie's naked form.

John lifted himself up, thinking back to last night. *What was I thinking?* He thought as he pulled his pants on.

He had been thinking about her. He wanted to comfort her in some way. He had to admit to himself that he wanted to be closer to her. She was so fragile...so beautiful...

He watched as she started to stir. She stretched herself, and she opened her eyes.

"Good morning, Maggie." John said to her, his hand caressing her hair.

Maggie's face was drowsy, but that quickly turned into recognition of the previous night.

"Oh...John...I don't think...," she stammered.

John shook his head.

"Maggie," he told her, leaning in close and kissing her lips. "I don't want you to feel ashamed about anything."

Maggie blushed. He loved looking at her when she blushed.

John stepped up from the bed and reached for his shirt. Suddenly, he heard a knock at the door.

"Rylund!" he heard Captain Orvis' voice say. "I came to check on you."

John looked at Maggie. Maggie shook her head.

"No use putting it off, Maggie," John told her simply.

Maggie thought for a moment. She nodded.

John walked over to the door and opened it up.

"Good morning, Captain," John said to him.

"Morning, Rylund!" Captain Orvis said to him. "How are you feel..."

Captain Orvis had noticed Maggie lying in the bed under the covers. He also noted John standing there bare-chested.

"May I come in?" he asked John sharply.

John stepped aside. He knew what was coming.

Captain Orvis walked inside, and John shut the door behind him.

"Captain Orvis," John began, "We..."

"Sit down, Rylund," Captain Orvis told him.

John walked back to his bed, and he sat down next to Maggie. She had retrieved her blouse, but she still sat under the covers of the bed.

Captain Orvis paced back and forth for several moments. Then, he spoke.

"I cannot stress enough the importance of your mission with M.A.D.," Captain Orvis began. "The protection of the colony is the number one priority."

He stopped and paced for a few moments more.

"I also understand that, at the end of the day, we are still human," he continued. "I certainly have no right to tell two grown adults that they cannot....be together."

Captain Orvis stopped at those words. The awkwardness of the moment was felt by all. John and Maggie glanced at each other.

John was the first to speak up. "I feel I can speak for both of us," he said firmly. "Maggie and I understand the mission at hand. Both of us want to defend and protect the people who live in this colony."

Maggie nodded at his words.

"This kind of relationship that you two are engaging in jeopardizes our mission!" Captain Orvis said sternly. "I cannot allow the two of you to..."

John stood up and stared the Captain straight in the eyes.

"I understand our mission," John said firmly. "And so does Maggie."

Maggie said nothing. Her face was tense.

63

Captain Orvis stared at John. He turned his eyes to Maggie. Her eyes were steady as well. He let out a sigh and rubbed his head. It had been throbbing terribly that morning.

"Very well," he resigned. "But I am still not pleased with this turn of events. I don't expect any diversion from duty. Understood?"

"Yes sir!" John and Maggie said.

"Dr. Cullen," Captain Orvis said. "I will be announcing at breakfast your appointment into M.A.D. Please wear your jumpsuit so you'll be recognized."

Captain Orvis then turned and walked towards the door, opening it. "I'll see you two at breakfast," he said.

And, with a nod, he left, slamming the door behind him.

John let out a sigh. "Well, that went better than I thought it would," John said cheerfully. "Don't you think so, Maggie?"

Maggie was getting her jumpsuit on. The blue stripes soon ran down her sides. She stood up alongside him. She nodded.

"You do look wonderful, you know that?" John said to her with a smile.

Maggie looked down at herself. She looked back at him.

"Well, gray is not exactly my color...," she said, raising an eyebrow.

Then, they both broke into laughter. It felt good.

After a few moments, Maggie said: "You know he is right."

John stopped his laughter and looked at her.

"Our duty has to come first, John," Maggie said to him.

John stayed silent for a moment. Then, he nodded.

"Have I put you in an awkward position?" he asked her.

"No," Maggie replied simply. They held hands together in front of themselves. Maggie glanced at John's wedding band.

"How about you?" she asked him.

John eyed his wedding band.

"I miss Evelyn every day," he told her. "I truly do. I wish none of this had happened..."

Maggie could see tears forming in his eyes. She brought her hand up and wiped them away – just as he had done for her last night.

"So do I," she told him softly. "But, here we are."

John nodded. He looked up at her and smiled.

"Thank you," he told her.

64

And with that, they both left for the Great Chamber.

Chapter 14

"...and so, Dr. Cullen entered the M.A.D," Captain Orvis finished.

Chatter broke out in the Great Chamber. Many people started cheering thanks. Captain Orvis looked over the assembled colonists, while John and Maggie seated behind him did the same.

Some of the colonists shouted out:

"An attack by the ocean?!" "Great job Dr. Cullen!" "Dr. Cullen isn't a fighter!" "She's a woman!" "Why wasn't anyone else picked?!"

Maggie face flushed at the insults. John looked to her and mouthed *stay calm*. She took a deep breath and calmed herself.

Captain Orvis held up his hands. Eventually, after some more grumbling, the colonists did quiet down.

"As I explained," Captain Orvis said evenly, "time was a factor. The enemy attack force was upon us, and we had no time to select candidates from the colony. Dr. Cullen offered up her skills, and, if not for her actions, we would all be dead."

He said that last word with finality. The colonists were silent.

"I expect the colony to give the same respect to Dr. Cullen that you give to Mr. Rylund," Captain Orvis said.

Muttering continued throughout the Great Chamber. Eventually, the muttering slowed down and stopped. People nodded throughout the crowd.

"Dismissed," Captain Orvis said to them all. "I think it's time we all had some breakfast."

The assembled colonists got up from their seats and lined up for the breakfast meal. Captain Orvis turned to John and Maggie, and, with a wave, dismissed them as well.

***

A short time later, Captain Orvis went to sit down at one of the empty tables.

"Good morning, Captain!" he heard a familiar voice say. He looked and saw Isaac striding towards him. "How are you this morning?"

"I have to admit it's been a rough few days, but I'll manage." Captain Orvis replied. After shaking his hand, Isaac sat down across from him.

"I saw your speech," Isaac said. "Nice comeback at the end."

Captain Orvis gave a smirk and bit into his breakfast.

"I guess John and Maggie are getting their trays now?" Isaac asked.

Captain Orvis stopped chewing and glared at Isaac.

"What?" Isaac said.

Captain Orvis swallowed his food. "Yes, they are getting their trays....*together*..."

Isaac looked at him quizzically. Captain Orvis explained very briefly about his encounter this morning. Isaac raised his eyebrows.

"I see," Isaac replied evenly. *Just as I figured*, he thought.

Captain Orvis shook his head and went back to eating.

After a few minutes, Captain Orvis asked: "How are the M.A.D. repairs doing?"

"The Fire Flyer has mostly completed repairs," Isaac told him. "And, as the Aqua Marine's subs suffered few losses, the repairs are already complete. Dr. Cullen was a good choice, after all."

Captain Orvis nodded, saying nothing.

Isaac decided it was time to change topics.

"So, I've been thinking," he told the Captain. "We've had both aerial and marine based attacks, but nothing over the ground."

Captain Orvis considered this for a moment. "That is true," he said. "We will have to plan for that."

"Way ahead of you," Isaac said with a smile. He leaned in close so they wouldn't be overheard. "I have been working on a third M.A.D. Machine. I still need to put some final tweaks on it this morning, but it should be ready soon."

Captain Orvis nodded, and, leaning back, noticed John and Maggie approaching. His gut did an involuntary clench.

"Good morning again Captain," John said as he and Maggie approached. "Good morning to you, Isaac."

John and Maggie sat down aside the two of them.

"Hey," Isaac said. "Great fight yesterday, Dr. Cullen. You really were a natural."

Maggie blushed. "Thank you Isaac," she said.

John smiled at her.

"I'm glad that jumpsuit fits you properly," Isaac said. "That was a stroke of luck."

John and Maggie started to eat breakfast along with them. John noted how the Captain sat silent.

After a few minutes, they heard a male voice from behind them call: "Morning folks!"

Maggie groaned.

Ricky and Naomi came striding towards the table with breakfast trays in their arms. They sat down: Naomi next to Maggie and Ricky next to her.

"So," Naomi said in wonder. "You joined the fight against the aliens?"

Maggie looked at her niece. She nodded.

"Wow," she said. "I...I...I don't know what to say."

"I'll be OK," Maggie told her. "The colony needed me. I knew what I was doing."

Maggie's eyes were tearing up. She hugged her niece.

Naomi broke off the hug, and she turned to look at Ricky.

"Wow," she told him. "Can you believe that? She's off fighting those aliens for us!"

"Yeah," he said. "You give it to 'em, Mags!"

Maggie scoffed.

"Oh, come on!" Ricky pleaded. "I gave you a compliment!"

"Maggie," John said to her sweetly. "We are at breakfast. Let's not start off the day like that."

Maggie looked at him and blushed. She resumed her eating.

68

The exchange had caught Naomi by surprise. "What's all this about, Maggie?" She said to her aunt curiously, looking back and forth between them.

Maggie stayed silent. Ricky was smirking.

"That blush can only mean one thing...," he said, smirking at John.

John noticed and glared back at him.

Isaac hadn't really been paying attention. He looked up from eating and saw the stares and smirks.

"Um...," he said. "Is something wrong..."

"Nothing is wrong," Captain Orvis interrupted sternly, surprising them all.

Captain Orvis noticed them staring at him. He coughed.

"Ahem," Captain Orvis said. "Rylund, you should head over to Security. Mr. Hall would like to have a word with you in regards to his duty rosters."

"He never could handle it by himself," John said shaking his head.

"Dr. Cullen," Captain Orvis said, turning to her, "as to your workload in the medical offices..."

"...I'll go and speak with Dr. Duncan," she assured the Captain.

"Very well," Captain Orvis said.

John and Maggie nodded and, finishing their meals, stepped up and left the table.

Ricky and Naomi exchanged glances. Ricky left after John, and Naomi left after Maggie. Captain Orvis watched them go off in their respective directions.

"I'm going to go and do the final tests for the M.A.D., Captain," Isaac said. He stood up and headed off to his lab.

Captain Orvis sat alone for a few moments. He could feel another headache coming on, and he started rubbing his forehead. Eventually, he picked himself up and left the Great Chamber as well.

***

"John!" Ricky called down the corridor.

John stopped and turned around. He could not imagine what this boy wanted with him.

69

"Hey," Ricky said, catching up. He smacked John on the shoulder. "I just wanted to say I thought you picked well."

John looked at him with a puzzled expression. "Picked what exactly?" he asked him.

"You know...Maggie," he said, chiding him. "Was she good last nig...OOOFF!"

The wind came out of Ricky's lungs quickly as John grabbed him by his jacket and slammed him into the wall. John put his face in front of Ricky's. Ricky's face was pale in fear.

"Don't...you...ever...speak...like...that...about...Maggie!" John said, saying every word fiercely.

"HEY...N-NO PROBLEM MAN!" Ricky said, his voice quivering. "I respect you and her! An..and don't worry! I treat Naomi right too! I...I just wanted to tell you it was cool..."

John held him there for several seconds. Then, John let go of Ricky and walked away to the security offices, while Ricky stood there trembling and panting.

Chapter 15

Naomi ran down the corridor after her aunt.

"Maggie!" she called.

Maggie stopped in the hall and turned back to her niece.

"I still don't like him," she told her flatly.

"I know you don't like Ricky," Naomi said to her. "I just wanted to tell you...I'm really proud that you're my aunt. Dad would have been proud of what you're doing."

Maggie was stunned at the mention of her brother. She felt her eyes start to water. "Thank you, Naomi," She said.

Then, Naomi said what else was on her mind.

"You spent the night with John, didn't you?" Naomi asked confidently.

Maggie's face went from compassion to shock and embarrassment.

"W-well....," Maggie stammered. "I needed someone last night..."

Maggie decided to confide in her. "Naomi, I do have to get to the infirmary," she said. "Walk along with me, and I'll explain everything..."

***

In the medical offices, Dr. Duncan was busy talking with the other doctors on the scheduling. He held out a large planning chart before him.

"And since Dr. Cullen won't be part of the rotation of on-call doctors...," he said. He paused and scratched his chin. "Dr. Trent and Dr. Knowles will take this shift here and here."

Maggie and Naomi had just reached the entrance to the medical offices. They said their goodbyes and Naomi walked off to the Agro sector. As Maggie entered, the assembled doctors turned in surprise. They broke out in smiles and offered her congratulations on her appointment to the M.A.D.

"Thank you," Maggie told them, she broke into a smile. "Thank you all."

Dr. Duncan waited until the doctors had finished their adulation, then he approached her directly.

"May I see you in my office?" he asked her.

Maggie nodded, and she followed him down the hallway. They reached his office door, and he closed it behind him. They sat down in his conference chairs.

He took a deep breath and said: "I know nothing can change that you're in the M.A.D. now. But, I am worried for you." He looked at Maggie with a caring expression on his face.

Maggie groaned. "Dr. Dun...HERMAN!" she said in frustration.

Dr. Duncan jumped in his chair.

"We've been over this!" she yelled at him. "I'm just your colleague, not your....ANYTHING!"

Dr. Duncan's face flushed red.

"And don't even try to deny it!" Maggie told him fiercely. "It's been that way from day one with you! You just don't know when to quit!"

Maggie stopped her tirade. She took several deep slow breaths. Dr. Duncan eyes were welled with tears.

Maggie had seen this before, too. *Enough is enough*, she thought.

"That's how it is," she said flatly. "Now, I would like to talk with you about my scheduling here. I know my M.A.D. duties will..."

She trailed off as Dr. Duncan got up and walked behind his desk. He sat back down and stared at Maggie.

"You were with Rylund last night, weren't you?" he asked

simply.

Maggie gasped. "How did you..."

"I went looking for you last night after I left the M.A.D. Bay," he told her. "I couldn't find you in your office or in your quarters. And then, when I went to breakfast this morning, who do I see you in line with? *Rylund!*"

Dr. Duncan slammed his hands onto his desk and sat up from his chair. He strode out of his office.

"HERMAN!" Maggie yelled after him. "Where are you going!?"

***

In the security offices, John and Mr. Hall were finishing up the scheduling changes.

"I put Pierce on the lower level," Mr. Hall was explaining. "But, he never works well with Trevor."

"Yes, I've dealt with Trevor before," John said, chuckling. "Put him with George. They tend not to bicker as much."

Mr. Hall nodded, making the note on his chart.

"So, how is Dr. Cullen fairing in this whole M.A.D. business?" Mr. Hall asked him.

John thought for a moment. He had known Joseph Hall for years in the Air Force. He knew he could keep secrets.

"Dr. Cullen is doing fine, Joseph," he answered. "She was a bit shaken up. She came to see me that evening."

Joseph looked up at his old friend. He saw how John was smiling.

"You mean you and...," Joseph said, trailing off.

John did not respond to the statement. He liked to let Joseph put things together.

"But," Joseph said. "What about Evelyn?"

John's face fell. His eyes went to his wedding band.

"I know you still miss her," Joseph said.

John breathed hard, keeping himself calm.

"I should have been there for her," John said.

"You were on duty, she knew that," Joseph countered. "The guy broke in and..."

Suddenly, they both heard the sounds of commotion outside

Joseph's office.

"LET ME IN!" someone roared.

Joseph and John looked at each other.

Suddenly, the office door was flung open, and Dr. Duncan stood there red faced. Several security personnel stood behind him. They had attempted to stop him, but Dr. Duncan's fury had carried him past them.

"YOU!" he shouted, pointing at John. "YOU STAY AWAY FROM MAGGIE!"

John's anger boiled. He stood up.

"And what if I don't?" he answered quietly, his eyes staring down Dr. Duncan. He involuntary flexed his arm muscles.

Dr. Duncan's face paled. He had forgotten just how strong and imposing John was up close.

After a moment, Dr. Duncan took a step back, lowered his arm, and walked briskly out of the security offices.

Chapter 16

Deep in his laboratory, Dr. Isaac Torre was busy at his computer – putting the finishing touches on the final M.A.D. for the colony's defense – the Dirt Driller.

The tank would be complete reinforced steel – again from the salvaged alien crafts. He had created a tank set that used diamond reinforced drill bits and the ability to fire heat lasers from the tips of said bits.

He adjusted his glasses and looked at the final schematics and programs again. He was brilliant, but, it never hurt to look over things twice.

He wondered to himself what man or woman would pilot this final savior for humanity. The Fire Flyer and Aqua Marine had found their pilots through volunteers. Would there be time to pick one from the colony like John Rylund? Or would circumstance force the choice, like in the case of Maggie Cullen.

He looked over at a stand nearby and saw the M.A.D. Black – the Dirt Driller's control device. Who would end up using it?

Only time would tell...

Ricky had walked from his encounter with John still shaking. He wasn't much of a fighter – if he was honest with himself, John could kick his ass up and down if he wanted.

He made a note of not trying to discuss sex encounters with John again.

He walked through the hallways wondering what to do that day. The first thought that came to him was that he had to find some kind of job for Naomi to stay with him. But, he did wonder what he could do.

He passed by a janitor in the corridor. *No, way.* He thought to himself. *I am not reducing myself to being a janitor.*

*I could work as a cook in the kitchens...*except I don't know how to cook.

I could work in the Agro department – then I could work with Naomi all day...

...but that means I'd have to...tend to plants...that don't talk...or move...how boring...

Damn...this is harder than I thought.

He knew that Naomi would be busy most of the day with her duties at the Agro sector, so spending some time with her would have to wait until tonight...

...*maybe she'll spend the night with me again,* he thought. *I still got it.*

Isaac...I wonder what Isaac is up to? He thought. He changed his direction and headed towards where Isaac's laboratory was. Usually, Isaac's lab was off limits to all but high end personnel, but he was his bud. He knew that he would let him in to chat it up for a bit.

As he strode down the hall, he noticed Captain Orvis approaching. He gave a smile.

Captain Orvis held up his hand for him to stop.

"You know...Ricky, is it?" he asked him as Ricky nodded. "Most folks tend to say 'Good Morning, Captain' or salute. I am the one in charge here."

Ricky smiled broadly. "Yeah, I know you're in charge." Ricky said. And with that, Ricky walked past him towards Isaac's lab.

Captain Orvis turned and watched him walk away. *What an arrogant little brat,* he thought to himself. He continued off to the medical sector – his original destination. His head was pounding.

As he strode down the corridor, he couldn't help recalling the run in with Ricky. *Boy has a lot to learn,* he thought.

***

Maggie sat at her office desk looking over some patient charts. She heard a knock at her open door and looked up.

"Captain Orvis!" Maggie said hurriedly, standing at once from her desk chair. "What can I do for you?" Inside, she wondered if she was going to be berated for this morning again.

"At ease, Dr. Cullen," he told her. He noted how she visibly relaxed "I'm actually here for my own health this time. Unfortunately, I cannot seem to locate my assigned physician, Dr. Duncan."

"Dr. Duncan left the offices this morning and hasn't been seen since," Maggie said flatly. She was still furious over his behavior.

"I see," Captain Orvis said thoughtfully.

"Was there anything I could do for you?" she asked him.

Captain Orvis sat down at the chair across from her. She sat down as well.

"I've been having some terrible headaches lately," he told her. "I have been suffering from some awful migraines the past few nights as well."

Maggie thought to herself for a moment. "I assume basic medicines haven't really helped?" she asked him.

"No," he told her. "I was recommended those remedies the previous visit I had. I was wondering if I had come down with something more serious. Would you be willing to check me more thoroughly?"

"Of course," she told him, and she led him off to one of the examination rooms.

After a few moments of checking some basic vitals – blood pressure, breathing, and lipids – she came to a decision.

"I'd like to get an X-Ray of your skull, if you're willing," she told him.

Captain Orvis' eyebrows tensed. "What are you thinking, Dr. Cullen?" he asked her.

"I just want to check something," she told him gently. "Right this way."

***

77

Isaac jumped in his desk chair. There was a loud pounding at the door to his laboratory.

Who could that be? He wondered.

He walked over and checked his camera feed. He opened the lock and slid the door open.

"Ricky!" Isaac said hurriedly. "What are you doing here?"

"I just came to drop by. See how things were going," he said. "Can I come in?"

Isaac groaned. "You know, Ricky...I really have things to do...," Isaac said to him seriously.

"You could use company couldn't you?" Ricky told him hopefully.

Isaac could see it was useless to try and defer Ricky. "Fine, come in!" he told him.

Ricky strode inside Isaac's lab. Isaac shut the door.

"I could get in so much shit for letting you in here!" Isaac scolded him. He walked over and sat down at this desk again, looking over the algorithms on the screen. *Sometimes,* he thought to himself, *I wish I hadn't brought him here.*

"When has anything bad happened when I visit?" Ricky asked. "Besides, I provide you with someone to spend some time with!"

Isaac didn't respond.

"Oh, fine! Be that way!" Ricky scoffed.

Ricky walked about the room and gazed at the large pictures of schematics here and there.

"What are these? Tanks?" Ricky asked Isaac, calling over his shoulder.

Isaac turned to face him. Seeing Ricky's interest in his inventions, he decided to engage the topic.

"Yeah, my newest invention – the Dirt Driller, and its respective mini-tanks," he told Ricky proudly.

"The *Dirt Driller?*" Ricky said, looking at him with an eyebrow raised. "That's the name?"

"I called the jet the Fire Flyer and the submarine the Aqua Marine," Isaac countered. "What's wrong with a tank being called the Dirt Driller?"

Ricky laughed out loud. "You can name 'em!" he said chuckling loudly.

Isaac rolled his eyes. *I liked it when I thought it up,* he thought to himself.

Ricky had walked over to a platform upon which sat a small device with a screen that resembled a calculator.

Ricky picked it up to examine it. "Hey, Isaac, what is this?" he asked.

Isaac turned toward Ricky and his face paled: "NO! DON'T TOUCH THAT!!!" he shouted...

...as the screen came to life and lights and data flashed across the screen of the device. Ricky stared at it in wonder. A moment later, the screen read the words: Ricky Plik, M.A.D. Black – Dirt Driller Pilot.

"Whoa, it knows me!" Ricky said cheerfully. "Neat trick. What's an M.A.D. Black?"

Isaac's face was chalk white.

"Isaac, you alright?" Ricky asked him.

At that moment, red lights went off the laboratory and alarms blared.

"Oh no! The aliens are back!" Isaac said, turning to his screen and tapping buttons quickly. "They've brought another attack force!"

Ricky came up behind him.

"Again? Thank god John and Mags got that under control." Ricky said.

Isaac scowled. "It's no good this time. It's not an air assault or an ocean attack...it's a ground force."

Isaac stood up and grabbed Ricky. "You need to come with me, RIGHT NOW!" he told him sternly.

***

Maggie was in the developing chamber for the X-Rays. She grabbed the film of the Captain's X-Ray. It would take just a few moments for it to develop.

"RED ALERT! RED ALERT!" the loud speaker chimed.

Maggie left the film, and stepped out of the room. She found Captain Orvis gathering himself together.

"Get yourself ready, Dr. Cullen," he told her, rubbing his forehead. "Head to the M.A.D. Bay. I'll check back with you on the

79

X-Ray results later. Rylund should be heading to the M.A.D. Hangar as we speak!"

Maggie nodded to him as he left, pulling out his communicator.

"I want all personnel down in the security barracks! NOW!" he barked.

Before she left, Maggie headed back to the X-Ray room. She pulled up the film, and she set it up on the view screen to look at later. She was about to turn away and head off when something on the film caught her eye.

Oh no, she thought.

Chapter 17

"I HAVE TO DO WHAT!?" Ricky yelled as he followed Isaac down to the lowest level of the colony. Red lights were flashing all around and alarms were going off.

"You have to pilot the Dirt Driller to defend the colony!" Isaac told him as they passed through some more doors.

"Why can't it be someone else again!?" Ricky asked in panic.

"You touched the M.A.D!" Isaac said. "It HAS to be you! Its D.N.A. locked onto you now! We don't have a choice!"

In his heart, Isaac wished it could be someone else. However, he had coded the M.A.D. himself. The only person who could use the M.A.D. was the first person who touched it. The D.N.A. lock made it so only a D.N.A. match would work for the device's activation. Damn his genius.

How would he explain this to Captain Orvis? To John? To Maggie? Hell, to everyone!? Ricky was certainly not the best choice...hell, he wasn't even a good choice! What would they all think? He certainly remembered how Maggie felt about him...

They had finally reached a massive chamber at the bottom of the colony. Isaac flipped a switch.

"This is the M.A.D. Bunker," Isaac said. He pointed with his finger: "...and there is the Dirt Driller!"

Inside the massive room stood a large, black-colored tank. Attached to the front of a set of large cone shaped drills – the center of the three was the largest. All about the Dirt Driller were several mini tanks – all sharing the same general design. A platform led up to the entrance of the tank.

"Here, catch!" Isaac said, as he threw Ricky something.

Ricky caught what appeared to be a gray towel. Unfolding it, he realized it was a gray jumpsuit like John and Maggie's – this one with black stripes down the sides.

"I have to wear this?" Ricky asked, examining it. "It's not really my style..."

"JUST PUT IT ON!" Isaac roared at him. "When you get back, I want you to look the part!"

Ricky jumped. Isaac had never yelled like that before. Ricky stripped down and pulled the jumpsuit on. It actually fit quite well.

That should gain him some creditability when he gets back. Isaac thought. *If he gets back.*

"Now, get in there!" Isaac yelled. He was already sitting at a console nearby.

Ricky jogged over to the platform and climbed up. He approached the entrance door.

"Uh," Ricky called to Isaac. "How do I...drive this thing..."

"GET IN!" Isaac roared again.

"OK! OK! I'M GOING!" Ricky said.

Ricky got close to the door and watched it slide open. The M.A.D. Black in his pocket was humming. He reached in and grabbed it with his hand. He saw the screen had lit up and kept it out.

He walked inside the Dirt Driller's interior. The inside was not as large as he had thought. Actually, it was quite cramped. He was just able to squeeze himself into the chair at the front. The glass windshield showed him the entrance door to the bunker.

"Now, put the M.A.D. into the console slot I designed." Isaac said to him.

Ricky looked at the console and found the slot that Isaac told him about. He pushed the M.A.D. Black into the slot and watched as it lit up. The screen on the console showed the Dirt Driller and all the other mini tanks coming to life.

"Pull the helmet on!" he heard Isaac say through what sounded like a radio.

He looked up and saw the helmet just above him. He grabbed it and pulled it down. As he felt it settle into place, he could hear and feel some wires and prongs going into his hair.

"ISAAC! WHAT IS THIS!?" he yelled out.

"It's alright!" he heard Isaac say. "They are attaching to your skull..."

"MY SKULL!" Ricky yelled again. "WHO SAID ANYHING ABOUT STUFF GOING INTO MY SKULL!?"

Ricky heard a frustrated groan on the other end of the static. Then, he heard the bunker door in front of him starting to creak open.

"Uh...now what?" Ricky said.

"Get ready!" Isaac said. "I'm opening up the bunker door! Get ready to fight off the alien tanks!"

"FIGHT TANKS?!" Ricky said nervously. The large door on the wall in front of him opened up and the sunlight shined inside.

Ricky stared out the windshield of the tank and looked out into the field surrounding the colony. Sure enough, enemy tanks and machines were approaching on the colony fast. Also, Ricky could see the same images appearing on the radar on his console.

"Oh boy...," Ricky said tentatively. *How do I make this thing move forward?* He thought. As he did so, the tank began to lurch forward in a steady roll.

"Alright," Ricky said, gritting his teeth. "Time to get this show on the road."

Ricky watched as the Dirt Driller rolled forward and out of the bunker along with the other mini tanks.

"Ricky," he heard Isaac say through static. "You may want to get your tanks in some kind of formation or something..."

"Oh, right," he replied. "How do I do that?"

"DAMN YOU!" Isaac shouted. "JUST THINK IT! LIKE I TOLD YOU!"

Ricky jumped in his seat. *Geez, my first day dude!* But, he did think about a long line of tanks. Sure enough, all the mini tanks lined up along side of him creating a line of tanks approaching the enemy force.

"Well?" Ricky said aloud. "What are we waiting for? FIRE!"

After shouting the last word, he watched as all the tanks began firing the heat lasers that Isaac had told him about. He saw the red hot beams shoot across the distance and blow up several of the oncoming tanks.

"YEAH!" Rick yelled. "Take that, scum bags!"

The enemy tanks soon began to fire back upon Ricky's tanks. He felt the explosions around him as the tanks were rocked with the attack.

"Oh!" Ricky yelled in excitement. "Tough guys huh? EAT THIS!"

Ricky made the tanks fire again upon the approaching tanks. He watched the screen and made his tanks fan out in an attempt to dodge the enemy fire.

Isaac watched the battle from the console in the M.A.D. Bunker. *He's recklessly*, Isaac thought. *But, it's not like he really knows battle tactics...*

"ISAAC!" he heard Captain Orvis say through the communicator. "What's going on? Where are you?"

"Oh no...," Isaac moaned. *Here we go.*

After a deep breath, he said: "Captain! I'm down in the M.A.D. Bunker on the lowest level of the colony. Come quickly! The battle is underway with an alien ground force!"

There was a slight pause. "I'm on my way!" Captain Orvis finally replied. "I'll contact Rylund and Cullen to come there as well!"

This is not going to be pretty, Isaac thought to himself.

Isaac continued watching Ricky battle in the Dirt Driller. A few moments later, Captain Orvis walked into the M.A.D. Bunker along with John and Maggie.

"Isaac, what's going on?" Captain Orvis said, hurrying over to where he sat at the console.

Isaac turned to face them. *No putting it off,* he thought.

"The new M.A.D. I constructed, the Dirt Driller as well as its mini tanks, is engaging the enemy tanks in a ground battle, Captain Orvis."

"Well, as usual Isaac, you've saved us again," Captain Orvis said to him. He looked at the battle on the screen. "Are you controlling the tanks from here?"

"Er...," Isaac hesitated. "No...not exactly..."

Captain Orvis stared at him. "Who's piloting the Dirt Driller then?" he asked him sternly.

John had noticed the discarded clothes nearby. He gestured to Maggie, and she gasped at the sight – recognition dawning on her face.

"I KNOW who clothes those are!" Maggie said with her voice full of fury.

Captain Orvis looked over, noticing the clothes pile for the first time.

"Isaac," he said turning his eyes back to his head scientist. "I'll ask you again, who is piloting the Dirt..."

"WHOO-HOOO!" Ricky shouted over the radio static.

John and Maggie gasped.

"YOU'VE GOT TO BE KIDDING!" John yelled.

"THAT IRRESPONSIBLE BUM!?" Maggie protested.

"ISAAC! YOU HAVE A LOT OF EXPLAINING TO DO!" Captain Orvis roared at him.

Isaac stood up from his chair, holding up his hands. Captain Orvis, John, and Maggie quietly stared daggers at him. He took a deep breath.

"Can this wait till later, please?" Isaac said, keeping his voice steady. "There is a battle going on!"

He had expected such a reaction. It didn't make it easier to take, though.

Isaac sat back down and examined the console and the ensuing battle. Ricky was actually holding his own pretty well for having never piloted a tank before. He had suffered losses, but, he was managing well enough.

"Ricky!" Isaac shouted to him. "Watch out! Some of those enemy tanks are digging under the ground to get around you!"

"I see it! I'm in control!" Ricky replied. "Down tanks! Intercept!"

Isaac watched as some of the mini tanks went down into the ground and clashed with the tanks under the ground.

"Why Ricky?" John said, his hands out in front of him. "WHY?!"

"I'd like to know that too!" Captain Orvis said sternly.

"He was here!" Isaac yelled from his chair.

"AND WHY WAS HE HERE?" Captain Orvis roared at him.

"Because...," Isaac hesitated, "...I let him in."

Captain Orvis brought his head down next to Isaac's. "We'll discuss this later," he said coldly.

"I'm all finished out here! I'll bring these tanks back!" Ricky yelled.

Isaac focused back on the console again. The enemy force was gone. "OK! I'm opening the bunker door for you!" he said.

The group watched as the M.A.D. Bunker door opened, and the Dirt Driller rolled back inside. The mini tanks followed with some parts of the enemy tanks – as well as pieces of his mini-tanks.

The Dirt Driller stopped in position next to the entrance platform. When the dust had settled around the tank treads, the door opened and Ricky stepped out smiling ear to ear. He held the M.A.D. Black in his hand.

"Isaac!" he yelled. "That was FUCKING amazing! I hope I can..."

He paused, seeing the rest of the group. "Oh, hi everybody!" he said cheerfully.

He gave the group of cheery wave as he climbed down, placing the M.A.D. Black in his pocket.

He jogged over to them and said: "Hey, how do you all think I...!"

… and Captain Orvis smacked him on the side of the head.

"My name is Captain Orvis!" he barked at him. "You are now part of Project M.A.D which protects the Terra Colony. You will address me as such!"

"Ow! What the hell was that for?" Ricky said, rubbing the side of his head.

"BECAUSE!" Maggie snapped at him.

John was staring hard at this foolish boy. "Do you realize what responsibility you have now?" John told him sternly.

"Geez, I think you'd all be happy with me!" Ricky protested. "I finally do something..."

Ricky paused.

"Wait!" he suddenly said. "I need to find Naomi!"

Ricky grabbed his clothes from the floor and ran out of the bunker.

"Wait!" Maggie yelled, as she began to chase after him. "What do you mean: 'I need to find Naomi!'? RICKY! GET BACK HERE!"

She stopped at the entrance door – Ricky was already out of sight.

Chapter 18

Maggie turned and came back to the others.

"He's gone!" she said furiously. She stared at Isaac.

"Ricky Plik," John said. "That...is who is going to help defend the colony?"

Isaac steeled himself. He said: "I know you're all mad with me..."

"That is an understatement," Captain Orvis interrupted, keeping his voice even. "You let Ricky in here. Why?"

"He wanted to hang out!" Isaac said exasperated. "He never caused problems before..."

Isaac slapped his hand over his mouth, realizing what he said.

Captain Orvis' eyes flared in anger.

"BEFORE?!" Captain Orvis roared at him. "How many times before!?"

"Does it matter?!" Isaac shouted. "I'm responsible for this. I get it!"

"Can it be reset?" Captain Orvis asked.

"What?" Isaac said, puzzled.

"The M.A.D.," Captain Orvis clarified. "Could you reset it to accept someone else?"

"No," Isaac said flatly. "Once someone touches the M.A.D, it locks their D.N.A. to the device. There is no way to reset it after that!"

"Well, this is a fine mess!" Maggie snapped. "Of all the

people in the colony – *him!*"

John took a deep breath. "Trust me Maggie," John said to her. "I don't like this development one bit." He shook his head in frustration. "I'll have to talk with the...boy...and I'll get him to understand the position he's been thrust into."

Captain Orvis was seething at this point. He eyed John. "SEE THAT YOU DO, RYLUND!" he barked. "I WILL NOT HAVE PLIK RUINING THIS ENTIRE OPERATION AND ENDANGERING THE COLONY WITH HIS NONSENSE!"

They all watched as Captain Orvis began to rub his forehead and groan.

"Are you alright, Captain?" Isaac asked him.

"Just a headache, nothing serious," he replied.

"Oh dear," Maggie said, her face tense in worry.

"I need to talk to the colony," Captain Orvis said, rubbing his forehead still. "I'll have to let them know about this development."

"Before you do that, Captain," Maggie told him. "I'd like you to come back to the infirmary with me. I need to talk to you about something."

Captain Orvis met her eyes, seeing concern. "Very well," he said. "We'll have to make it quick."

He walked out of the M.A.D. Bunker.

Isaac and John eyed her curiously. They had watched her expressions with interest.

"Don't worry," she said. "I just want to show him something."

Maggie left to follow the Captain. John, with a look of malice at Isaac, left to find Ricky.

Isaac breathed a sigh of relief. *That went better than I thought.*

Ricky ran through the hallways of the colony. He had dropped off his clothes at his quarters, and he had gone as fast as he could to find Naomi and tell her the good news.

There is no way she can say I don't have a job now! I'm kicking alien ass! He thought to himself.

He passed many colonists on his way and gave them his best smile ever. Many hailed him as they noticed his jumpsuit. Some others stared at him with mouths gaping.

Come on people, he thought. *I'm a hero now!*

As he made a turn in the corridor...

SLAM!

Ricky tumbled over someone, and they both crashed into the floor.

"OH! Hey sorry!" he said, as he helped the other man up. "Are you OK?"

"I'm fine," the other man said, standing and brushing himself off. "I'm f..."

Dr. Duncan finally got a look at the man who crashed into him.

"Ricky Plik!" he said in surprise. Ricky was one of his assigned patients. "Where are you..."

Dr. Duncan trailed off again as he noticed what Ricky was wearing.

"You're in the M.A.D?" he asked Ricky in a neutral tone.

"Oh, yeah!" Ricky said, admiring his jumpsuit. "Sweet, huh?"

"And...whose decision was this?" Dr. Duncan asked him.

"Well, I didn't really get *chosen*...," Ricky said unsteadily. "But, there I was. The aliens attacked, and I kicked some ass!"

Dr. Duncan gaped at him. "I see," he said. "Ricky, if will excuse me I have to find the Captain."

And with that, Dr. Duncan turned the corner and left him there. Ricky didn't see how red his face was getting.

   ***

Ricky finally reached the Agro sector. He looked around quickly and spotted Naomi at the far other end. He dashed down the aisles of plants, dodging around a few of the workers and various equipment.

He reached Naomi just as she spotted him bounding down towards her. She put down her tools just in time for him to pick her up. He spun her around in the air and kissed her.

"RICKY!" she said surprised. "WHAT ARE YOU..."

"YOU ARE COMING TO MY PARTY!" he declared to her.

She looked at him puzzled. She thought he had greater news...

...and then she noticed what he was wearing.

"Ricky!" she said with a start. "You're in the M.A.D?"

"I am!" he said cheerfully. He put her down and showed her his M.A.D. Black.

Naomi looked at him in wonder for a moment.

"This is a joke, right?" she said to him.

Ricky looked affronted. "Why would I lie to you? What, you think I made this jumpsuit and this thing to trick you?" He waved the M.A.D. Black in his hand.

"No! No!" she said. "I just...this is..."

"Aren't you happy for me?" Ricky said, putting on a sad face.

Naomi thought for a moment. *This whole situation was dangerous, or course. At least he was doing something useful. But, him? Still...*

Naomi finally settled herself. "Well, of course I'm happy for you!" she said.

"That's my girl!" Ricky said, smiling ear to ear. "Hey, I am starving. Fighting takes a lot out of a man. Care to join me for lunch?"

He offered her his arm.

Naomi glanced at the clock. "Well, my shift is just about up." She looked to Mr. Juniper, her supervisor, who gave her a nod. "I suppose I can make some time for you...unless you think you're all important now and don't have time for me, being a hero and all?"

Ricky looked at her admiringly. The sass was always something he loved about her.

And together, they walked from the Agro sector. Some of the other workers waved towards Naomi and Ricky as they passed by.

Things are looking up, he thought to himself.

Chapter 19

Ricky and Naomi arrived at the Great Chamber hand in hand. After gathering their trays, they went to sit down. Many of the colonists gave looks of wonder, while some of them offered an encouraging wave.

"Wow," Naomi said, looking around, "all this attention you're getting – can you handle it?"

"Sure I can!" he said cheerfully, sitting down at a table with her. "This won't be a big deal at all. Trust me!"

Naomi looked at him. She loved him, but even she knew he was gloating....just a bit.

"So," she asked him, how did it happen?"

"What?" he asked her, as he bite into his food.

She chuckled. "How did you get into the M.A.D?"

Ricky finished chewing and swallowed. He thought to himself for a moment and said: "Well, I was in the lab with Isaac. And, the aliens attacked again. Well...I was the only one there who could help...so...I volunteered."

Naomi raised an eyebrow. "You volunteered?" she said skeptically.

Ricky blushed. *Damn, she can read me like a book*, he thought. "OK, I was there...but I didn't exactly volunteer..."

In a hushed voice, he explained what had happened in the M.A.D. Bunker earlier.

Naomi burst into laughter. Some of the nearby tables turned

to look. Ricky joined in with her.

"You're joking?!" she said as their laughter died down. She brought her voice down to a whisper so she wouldn't be overheard.

"Honestly, leave it to you!" Naomi said quietly.

Ricky shrugged. "It turned out OK! I'll be taking care of things on the ground now. So, no one has to worry!"

Naomi smiled at him. "Alright," she said, eating some of her lunch for a few minutes. "What's it like in those things, anyway?"

"Well, like I said," he began. "I got this giant tank called the Dirt Driller..."

"The Dirt Driller?" she said with a smirk.

"Yeah, I thought the name was stupid too..."

"I HEARD THAT!" a voice snapped behind them. They turned and saw Isaac approaching.

"Oh, hey Isaac!" Ricky said, calling him over.

"Lay off about the name, already!" Isaac scolded him as he sat down.

Naomi chuckled. Isaac stared at her.

"I agree!" Naomi said to him with a smile. "What were you thinking?"

"I was thinking I built the damn things, and I could name them whatever I want!" Isaac said fiercely.

"Hey, it's cool Isaac," Ricky said, smiling at him.

Isaac scowled again and dug into his lunch.

"So, back to the battle you were gonna tell me about?" Naomi said.

"Oh right!" Ricky said. "So, I get into the tank, and I put the helmet on. And these wires come from the helmet and go into my skull..."

Ricky involuntarily checked his head quickly with his hands. A few welts were here and there.

"Eww!" Naomi said. "Wasn't that painful?"

"Not really," Ricky said. "So, the big door opens from the bunker..."

Naomi listened, enraptured with his story.

"So, I tell the tanks to go and shoot those machines here and here," Ricky said, indicating with his fingers positions on the table.

Ricky continued explaining the battle in such a way for a few minutes.

"You should have seen me, Naomi!" he said proudly. "I kicked some ass out there!"

"Not without losses," Isaac chimed in.

"Did you have to put a damper on my story?" Ricky told him.

Isaac sighed. "Alright, I admit you didn't do terribly," he said. "But, you were reckless out there!"

"I agree," a deep voice said nearby.

They turned to see John walking towards them with a tray in his hand.

"Hey John!" Ricky said to him. "Good to see you!"

"I'm glad I found you," John said, sitting down with them. "I wanted to have a word with you about being in the M.A.D."

Ricky sat puzzled for a moment. "About what?"

John sat back, taking a deep breath. "You really have no idea what you've gotten yourself into, have you?" John asked him. "You are..."

At that moment, sirens went off in the colony, and John's M.A.D started buzzing. Isaac's communicator went off as well. He pulled it out and examined it.

Security was already escorting the colonists towards the security barracks. Some of them looked to the table were John and Ricky were sitting. Ricky gave an encouraging wave.

"Don't worry!" he told them cheerfully. "We got this!"

John turned and glared at him in amazement. *Boy has a lot to learn*, he thought.

"What is it?" John asked turning back to Isaac. Ricky turned to look as well.

"It's another air assault!" Isaac said. "Also, those subs are back! Thank goodness all the repairs to your mini jets are finished!"

"I'll head to the M.A.D. Hangar!" John said, standing up. He turned to Ricky. "Ricky, we'll pick this up later!"

Ricky nodded. "Give 'em hell, John!"

John just shook his head, groaned, and ran off to the M.A.D. Hangar.

"I'll get a hold of Maggie!" Isaac said, as he headed off following John.

"Hey, what am I supposed to do!?" Ricky called after them. But soon, they were gone and out of sight, leaving Ricky and Naomi at the table alone.

Captain Orvis sat back in his chair.

"Tumor?" he said evenly, trying to maintain himself.

They were back in the Infirmary. Maggie had put up the X-ray she took earlier.

"Yes," she said, pointing. "This tumor on the top of your spinal cord may be benign. I'd like to do a biopsy as soon as possible."

For perhaps the first time, Glenn Orvis was lost for words.

"I like to be serious with my patients," Maggie said. "If this is cancerous, it is inoperable. Trying to remove something like that from so close to the brain and nerve stem is simply too risky."

Maggie looked at the Captain. His face was pale.

"I'm sorry, Glenn," she said finally.

"T…This...," Captain Orvis stammered. "This cannot be happening..."

The door to the exam room burst open, and Dr. Duncan strode inside, his face red with anger.

"THERE YOU ARE GLENN!" he roared to the Captain.

Captain Orvis looked up at him, trying to put up a stern visage.

"What the hell do you think you're doing putting Ricky Plik into the M.A.D?!" Dr. Duncan yelled. "First Maggie and now..."

"Dr. Duncan!" Maggie yelled back. "This is hardly the place for this...."

"OH NO, YOU DON'T!" Dr. Duncan fired back. "I am not being ignored this time! Captain Orvis is going to answer for this! I will not..."

"HERMAN, STOP IT!"

SLAP!

Maggie withdrew her hand from Dr. Duncan's face.

Dr. Duncan rubbed the side of his face. He looked at Maggie in shock and disbelief.

Maggie was breathing heavily. Captain Orvis had stayed silent, but he had jumped in his seat at Maggie's slap.

"Dr. Duncan," Maggie said evenly. "Look at that X-ray over there."

Dr. Duncan, confused, walked over to the X-ray on the wall. He studied it carefully for a moment.

In a flash, he realized what he was seeing.

He turned to look at Captain Orvis. He saw how he was trembling.

"Captain," Dr. Duncan said nervously. "I..."

At that moment, sirens and alarms went off. Maggie's M.A.D. Blue buzzed and the Captain's communicator went off as well.

"Captain!" Isaac said over the communicator. "The aliens are attacking from the air and the sea. Maggie, we need you in the M.A.D. Bay!"

"Roger that!" Maggie said into her M.A.D.

She looked towards the Captain. He seemed to gain back his nerve with the alien attack to occupy his thoughts.

"Let's get going!" Captain Orvis said. "They aren't going to stop for me, are they?"

And with that, Captain Orvis headed out of the infirmary.

Maggie gave Dr. Duncan one last scathing look, and she turned and followed the Captain.

Chapter 20

John arrived at the M.A.D. Hangar. He quickly climbed up into the Fire Flyer and locked the cockpit down. With the M.A.D. Red locked into the console, the helmet descended and the wires attached to his head.

Isaac had arrived with him and got onto the console station there. He began typing quickly.

"I have a link to the M.A.D. Bay and the Aqua Marine while I'm here," Isaac said over the radio link to John. "Can you hear me Maggie?"

"Yes!" they both heard her say over radio static. "I'm just starting up the Aqua Marine!"

John looked down at his console screen in the Fire Flyer. He could see his Fire Flyer and the mini jets. Additionally, he could see Maggie's layout and subs.

"Everyone, I'm here in the M.A.D. Bay to spot for Dr. Cullen!" Captain Orvis said. "Is everyone ready?"

"Ready here sir!" Isaac said from the M.A.D. Hangar.

"Ready!" John said from inside the Fire Flyer.

"Ready here!" Maggie said from inside the Aqua Marine.

"Let's get going!" Captain Orvis said.

In the M.A.D. Hangar, the door opened to reveal the attacking force of alien fighters. John took a deep breath and had his jets fire up.

In the M.A.D. Bay, the Aqua Marine submerged into the

water and joined the other mini-subs. It launched out as the approaching mini subs came into the radar's view.

The Fire Flyer shot out of the M.A.D. Hangar, and John began to fire his lasers onto the enemy aircraft. The mini-jets flanked him to create a sweep about him.

"Great start out there, John!" Isaac said.

"Yes, excellent!" Captain Orvis said. "Dr. Cullen?"

Maggie had forced her mini subs into a circle around her as before.

"I've set up the perimeter as before," she said to him.

"BLOCK THAT!" she suddenly shouted. Captain Orvis and Isaac watched as her pressure torpedoes intercepted enemy fire in the water.

John, having to focus on his flight and firing patterns, could not focus on his console to take direct notice.

"Maggie, a best offense is a good defense," he told her calmly. "But, you should try to pick them off as well."

"Easy for you to say!" she scolded him over the static. "You're not the one surrounded by the blackness of the water around you!"

John went silent for a moment. His mind focused on the fight as explosions were happening around him.

"Maggie," he said, speaking firmly. "You cannot think about the possibility of loss. You have to focus on what your mission is. Keep up defenses. Pick them off a bit at a time."

Maggie breathed heavy. "OK," she said. She watched as another torpedo fired towards her.

...and then another.

She fired off her torpedoes as fast as she could. A few of the shots managed to break her defense ring – the bubbling explosion shaking the tension of the water. The remnants of the mini-subs floated lifeless in the water.

"Drat!" Maggie shouted in frustration.

Up in the air, John was dodging enemy fire with flair. He had new formations for his mini-jets, and they were working better than he could have hoped.

Suddenly, he felt an impact on his tail-side. The impact rocked his cockpit.

"JOHN!" Maggie yelled from the Aqua Marine.

97

"DON'T WORRY ABOUT ME!" John said fiercely. "You have to focus on the subs!"

"John is right!" Captain Orvis said. "You have your own problems!"

"Oh, right!" Maggie said. She had lost focus there. She turned back to blocking the enemy fire of the subs.

"John, the mini-jets are their making repairs," Isaac said. "How is your stability?"

"Fine!" John said. His voice was full of tension.

"Maggie?" Isaac asked hurriedly.

"I'm alright, OH!" she yelled suddenly. An explosion rocked the waters. A few of her mini subs got struck again.

She sent her mini subs towards the alien force, having them fire their pressure torpedoes at full force. Many explosions went off near the enemy force. She checked her screen. *Gotcha*, she thought.

"Nice shot, Maggie," Captain Orvis said, rubbing his head. "Keep it up."

Maggie couldn't help hear the slight falter in his voice – and that he called her *Maggie* and not *Dr. Cullen*.

Up in the air, John was focusing as hard as he could.

"Seems like they learned some new tricks!" John said to them all, as he dodged another wave of enemy fire.

"Probably have learned from the previous battles," Isaac said. "You're doing fine though. Their numbers are falling!"

"Same down here, Isaac," Captain Orvis said. "Get those last ones then you're done Maggie."

Maggie focused her attention on the final few enemy subs. Enemy torpedoes fired back and a few more of her subs took losses. However, her shots managed to get through and the battle in the sea was over.

"Finally," Maggie said, her voice relaxed. "I'm bringing the Aqua Marine back in Captain."

"Good job, Maggie," Captain Orvis said, his voice sounding very weary. "I'll..."

His voice stopped. Maggie heard something like a crash in her earpiece.

"Captain?" Maggie asked over the radio as she brought the sub into dock.

In the air, John was finishing with the enemy crafts. He did one final circle about the colony. All the enemy craft were gone.

"All done up here!" John said. "I'm bringing myself in!"

Isaac nodded at his console. "Excellent work as usual, John. Captain?"

He heard no response. "Captain?" he repeated.

"MEDICAL TEAM TO THE M.A.D. BAY!" he heard Maggie yell over the intercom. "CODE ONE!"

Isaac got up from his console as John pulled the Fire Flyer into the Hangar. John stepped out.

"John!" Isaac yelled to him. "Code One!"

John face paled. "Let's go!" he shouted.

About an hour later, John, Maggie, and Isaac sat around the bed Captain Orvis was lying in.

"I'm fine," he told them.

"You were passed out in the M.A.D. Bay!" Maggie said. "You should be lucky I got back when I did!"

"What happened, exactly?" John asked her.

Maggie hesitated. She looked at the Captain. He nodded.

"When I took an X-Ray of the Captain earlier," she said. "I found this."

She put up the X-Ray she had taken earlier. She indicated the spot near the brain stem.

Isaac was the first to realize what was being shown. "It's a tumor." he said, dumbstruck.

"Yes," a man voice's said. Dr. Duncan walked into the room. His face was grim. "I performed a biopsy when I got him here. The tumor is malignant."

Captain Orvis' face paled. "How long do I have?" he said meekly.

"We don't know," Maggie said to him. Dr. Duncan agreed with a shake of his head.

"It won't be long, Glenn," Maggie said with finality.

Captain Orvis went silent. No one else said a word.

"John, I would like to ask you a favor," Captain Orvis said after a few moments.

"Yes, Captain?" John said.

"John," he said to him, taking a deep breath. "If I die, I want you to lead the colony as Captain in my place."

John was stunned by the request. Isaac and Maggie both were shocked as well. Dr. Duncan said nothing, but his fists clenched.

"Are you sure?" John asked the Captain.

"Positive," he replied. "I've been giving it thought. What would happen if I died? Who would lead the colony? I cannot think of anyone else I'd rather have with the job. The people love you. You are a symbol of strength for them. You also, in their minds, lead the M.A.D. force against the aliens. Do you accept this appointment?"

John leaned back. He thought about it for several moments.

"What do you all think?" John asked, turning to the rest of the group.

Isaac smiled. "I think you'd be a great Captain," he said.

Maggie just nodded simply.

John turned to look at Dr. Duncan.

"Well, Dr. Duncan," John asked him. "What are your thoughts?"

"As I seem to remember…," Dr. Duncan said, speaking slowly and deliberately. "…the charter of the Terra colony states that the Captain's position is only transferred through vote by the department chairs. And…"

…and," Captain Orvis interrupted darkly. "The acting captain may willingly transfer his duties to an appropriate candidate given witness and consent by acting department chairs. Are you saying you refuse this choice, Dr. Duncan?"

"I do," Dr. Duncan replied flatly, staring daggers at John.

"Well," Captain Orvis said, raising an eyebrow. "I'm afraid your objection is meaningless…"

"What do you mean?!" Dr. Duncan said, flustered.

Captain Orvis pointed to Maggie.

"As Maggie is a member of the M.A.D.," Captain Orvis explained, "her position is *above* yours, and, therefore, her consent *trumps* yours. So, my selection has been approved."

Dr. Duncan's face flushed red. He took several deep breaths, but said nothing.

"Well, John?" Captain Orvis said, turning back to him.

"Yes," John finally said. "I'll do it."

"Excellent," Captain Orvis said. "Also, I must ask that we keep my condition secret. There is no need to panic anyone. Of course, the department chairs should be told about my condition, as well as the choice for the leader. Maggie, if you could handle that?"

She nodded to him.

"Now, you two," Captain Orvis said, indicating John and Maggie, "Go get some rest. Isaac, you monitor the M.A.D. Repairs. We need them to be back at full force as soon as possible."

Captain Orvis stood up wearily. "I feel alright for the moment," he said, seeing their worried looks, "I'm heading to my quarters for now. Keep me up to date on the status of things, won't you Isaac?"

He nodded.

"Very well," Captain Orvis said. "Dismissed."

Chapter 21

In her quarters, Naomi waited patiently for Ricky. She hadn't seen him during dinner that night, so she hoped he would stop by her quarters.

After the all clear was given from the recent alien attack, she had headed back to the Agro sector (Ricky had wanted to tell all his friends the good news), and she had spent most of her day in awe and wonder.

Ricky – a part of the M.A.D?

She could hardly believe it. If it hadn't been for the fact that Ricky had told her exactly how it had happened – and that neither John or Isaac had refuted it – she would have thought he was pulling her leg.

The idea excited her – *her man a hero...*

...that would make Maggie shut up.

Suddenly, she heard a knock on the door. She walked over and opened it.

Ricky stood there. He grinned from ear to ear as he stood there before her. He was still wearing his gray M.A.D. jumpsuit.

"Hey," he said to her. "How are you doing?"

He stepped forward, and they embraced. He kissed her softly on the lips.

Damn he knows how to kiss, she thought.

She brought him inside the apartment. Ricky looked around. It looked as it did when he was there last. She had the simple artwork up on the walls, and her bed was still flanked by stuffed animals.

She brought him over to her bed. She sat down and patted the space next to her.

She looks beautiful tonight, he thought as he sat down.

Naomi flung her head, and her long blonde hair fell over her right shoulder. She fluttered her eye lashes at Ricky.

"So," she asked him sweetly, "Tell me more about this fight today. How do you make all the tanks fight? You mentioned wires in your head before..."

"Well," he began. "I'm inside the Dirt Driller tank. I have all the enemy tanks coming at me. I'm a little nervous I admit, but I decide to give it my best shot."

Naomi listened intently. She knew he was bloating things a bit, but she didn't care. She wanted to make him feel good.

"So, I just start thinking – and that's all you have to do. You just think about what you want the Dirt Driller and the mini-tanks to do, and they just do it. I have them make a huge line in front of me and have them start firing."

"Didn't they start to fire back?" Naomi asked, mocking fear.

"Well, yeah they did!" he said. "They fired lasers back at me, and a few of my tanks blew up around me. I didn't know if I'd make it. I thought I was gonna die, but I kept on at it."

Ricky continued his description of the battle. Naomi nodded and smiled at him.

"And...that's about it," he finished. "Boy, you should have seen the look on your face when I ran up and grabbed you in the Agro sector!"

Naomi smiled at him, and then she laughed.

"Oh, you are so full of crap!" she said, punching him in the shoulder.

"Hey, I didn't lie!" Ricky said to her.

"Oh really?" she said. "I talked to Isaac. He made it sound like you were hooting and hollering like a cowboy out there!"

Ricky blushed. Naomi smiled at him.

She brought her lips to his cheek and kissed him.

Then she whispered in his ear: "I like cowboys." And she kissed him again.

He turned and brought his lips to hers.

"I forgot to shower today...," she whispered to him.

They both stood up and walked to her shower stall.

***

John walked with Maggie down the hallways of the colony that evening. Dinner had been a quiet affair, as it had been a busy day.

They had been to visit the heads of the various departments to let them know of Captain Orvis condition, and of John's selection as successor. Both Mr. Hall and Mr. Juniper respected the choice made.

They walked towards John's quarters. John had agreed to escort Maggie to her quarters for the evening, as she was a bit shaky still from the day's events. But, his happened to be on the way.

"I noticed no sign of Dr. Duncan at dinner," John said to Maggie casually.

"He's probably off sulking," Maggie said, disgust in her voice. "Between you becoming Captain and me having to explain how Ricky became part of the M.A.D...."

Maggie trailed off.

"What did he do?" John asked her, tension filled his voice.

"Oh! He did nothing to me!" Maggie explained quickly. "He walked to his office and slammed the door. I don't know what to say to him anymore."

John nodded. *Dr. Duncan will be difficult when I become Captain*, he thought.

They finally reached the door to John's quarters.

"Maggie," he said, coming to a stop, "could you wait right here for just a moment? I want to get something."

She nodded.

John unlocked the door and went inside.

He had been preparing this for some time now. The conversation he had had with Mr. Hall had inspired him. He hurried quickly into his quarters.

A few years ago, he was out fishing in his old rowboat. He had gotten a fish on his line that had fought him hard. He pulled. He tugged. The boat rocked...

...and the fish got away with a snap..

104

He had pulled the line back in and examined the end. He wasn't sure how it happened, but the fish had snapped the barb clear off his lure. What remained of the lure was the red and blue colored fish designed to look like a minnow. He had placed it in his tackle box at that time, thinking he would get it fixed at some point. It was one of his favorites.

But, he never had. Just as well he didn't.

He grabbed his tackle box from inside his dresser and pulled it out. He had made something new out of the old lure.

He opened the tackle box and pulled out the lure – now a necklace made of out fishing wire. It had taken some time for the wire to smooth out and stop being roundish, but it had finally settled.

He replaced the tackle box and went back out to the hallway.

"This is for you," he said. And he handed her the necklace.

"Oh!" she said. "It's...beautiful."

Maggie wasn't the kind of woman who liked jewelry. This necklace was just a simple gesture of affection from John.

When was the last the last time I did things like that for Evelyn? John thought to himself as Maggie placed the necklace around her neck.

"I'm glad you like it," John said to her. "Now, I believe I was leading you to your quarters?" He extended his elbow out to her.

Maggie took his arm and off they walked.

Maggie waited for a few moments of walking to speak, checking that no one was around.

"How do you feel about being the Captain once Glenn dies?" she asked him.

John took a deep breath. "It will be difficult," he said, "what with my M.A.D. duties on top of it. But, I guess I don't have much of a choice."

"Yes, you did!" she said sharply. "You didn't have to accept the appointment!"

"I cannot find fault in his reasoning," he replied firmly. "The colonists look up to me, and they look to the M.A.D. to keep them safe. Who else can you think of that would do it?"

Maggie had no answer for that.

A few moments later, they arrived at Maggie's quarters.

"Thank you for walking me home," Maggie said warmly.

"It was my pleasure, my lady." he said to her.

Maggie opened her door up. She started to enter, and then she turned back to look at John.

"John," she asked him, "would you...stay with me tonight?" Her eyes glittered.

He nodded to her and smiled. That was not his intention that evening, but he was happy for it.

Chapter 22

John heard a beeping. That was the sound that woke him.

He turned to his left side. He saw Maggie laying there. He smiled.

He turned to his right to find the source of the beeping – his M.A.D. Red on the table.

The M.A.D. Blue next to it was beeping as well.

John picked his up.

"John!" he heard Isaac say. "Are you up?"

John yawned. "Ye..yes...I am," he replied. "What's going on?"

There was a pause.

"Glenn died last night," Isaac said simply. "Security found him still in his bed when he didn't do his rounds this morning."

John took a deep breath. *So, I'm Captain now*, he thought.

John turned to look at Maggie. She had woken up when the M.A.D.s went off. Her face was deep with sadness.

"Where is his body now?" John asked Isaac.

"The on-call medical team led by Dr. Duncan came to get the body," Isaac replied. "It's currently in the medical department."

"We'll need to have a funeral for him," John said, "I'll contact security this morning and have a time and place set up."

"Very well, Captain Rylund," Isaac said.

"Over and out," John said.

John sat the M.A.D. Red down and began to get dressed.

Maggie had already begun.

"How does it feel to be Captain Rylund?" Maggie asked him.

John shrugged. "Well, I don't feel any different. Do I look different?

Maggie walked over and kissed him. "You look just the same – if not better."

John smiled.

"I will need to go and talk to Ricky," John said, putting his M.A.D. Red into his pocket. "Our conversation got cut off yesterday with the attack. First though, I should go around and check in with the departments."

Maggie gave him a kiss. "Have a good day, Captain Rylund." she said to him. "I'll be heading to breakfast. I hope I get a chance to see you there. You can't do this all on an empty stomach."

"Agreed," he said to her, and he left.

    ***

John moved at a brisk pace down the colony corridors.

He stopped first at the security offices to speak with Mr. Hall.

"Well, good morning John," Mr. Hall said to him, standing up from his desk. "Or should I say good morning Captain Rylund?"

Mr. Hall gave him a salute.

"At ease, Joseph," John said to him. "I'll not be imposing such rigid protocol with you. I wanted to discuss setting up a funeral for Captain Orvis..."

They both agreed that the funeral would be planned for later that week. Also, word was to spread down to all sectors of John's position as Captain through security.

After that, John went down to visit the body in the medical department. As he entered, he noticed Dr. Duncan talking with his nurses.

"Good morning, Dr. Duncan," John said formally.

Dr. Duncan turned to John and hesitated for a moment. "Good morning...Captain Rylund."

John nodded to him. "Where is the body?" he asked simply.

"Follow me," Dr. Duncan said, and walked down the hallway with John following him.

The last door held the colony's morgue. Dr. Duncan led the

way inside and showed John Glenn's corpse lying on a table. John nodded, and Dr. Duncan led the way out.

"We are planning a funeral in the next few days," John explained. "Please keep the body as preserved as possible."

Dr. Duncan nodded silently as John left.

The remaining rounds didn't take much more time. John arrived at the Great Chamber in time for breakfast, and he found Maggie waiting for him.

"We're planning a funeral for Captain Orvis later this week," he explained to Maggie as he ate. "That will give people a chance to show their respects."

Maggie nodded. She seemed lost in thought.

"What's wrong Maggie?" John asked her.

"Have...you seen Naomi anywhere?" she asked him curiously, her head looking about.

"No, I haven't," he replied, thinking on it. "In fact, when I was visiting Mr. Juniper in the Argo sector, I didn't see her there either. I still need to talk to Ricky – I'll ask him if he has seen her."

Maggie smiled. "Thank you for your efforts, Captain."

***

After finishing his meal, John went looking for Ricky. He went to his quarters, and upon knocking, heard no response.

There is only one place he would be then, he thought.

He made a march to where Naomi's quarters were.

He stopped at the door and took a deep breath. He knocked.

"Just a minute!" he heard a sleepy male voice say.

After a moment, Ricky opened up the door shirtless. His hair was frazzled. He must have just gotten up.

"I found you," John said to him. "You missed breakfast."

"Aw, sorry," Ricky said through a yawn. "Was a busy night...and a late morning."

"May I?" John asked him, gesturing inside.

"Oh, sure John!" he said, and led him inside.

John walked pasted Ricky's shirtless form and took in the form of Naomi lying under the sheets.

He paused upon seeing her. *This must be how the Captain felt*, he thought. *At least the kid put his pants on.*

John also noticed the trays of food sitting near the bedside.
"Ordering in?" John asked them.

"No!" Naomi said, scowling. "I went to get food for breakfast, and I brought it back here."

"Nothing wrong with that, it is John?" Ricky said happily. "A little breakfast in bed for the new M.A.D. member!"

Ricky puffed out what little of a chest he had.

"Sit down, Ricky," John said sternly.

Ricky frowned. He sat down in a chair next to the bed, and John stepped up next to the bed to address them both.

"Well," John said, standing up straight. "The first thing I need to let you both know is that, if you haven't heard, Captain Glenn Orvis is dead."

Ricky's eyes widened. "Oh man," he said soberly, shaking his head. "That sucks."

"How did it happen?" Naomi asked sadly.

John gave a brief synopsis of the events leading to Captain Orvis' death.

Ricky and Naomi said nothing.

"It would interest you to know," John said facing Ricky directly. "That I am the new Captain of the Terra colony. Effective immediately."

Ricky seemed to perk up. "Well, there ya go, John!" he said, smacking him on the shoulder. "Congrats on the promo!"

John stared at the boy. *Time to buckle down,* He thought.

"That also means I am your commanding officer," John said darkly. "You will address me as 'Captain' or 'Sir'."

"Well, sir yes sir!" Ricky said, making a mock salute.

Well, its a start, John thought.

"I wanted to tell you about the M.A.D. battle yesterday," John said. He glanced at Naomi.

"Anything you tell him he will tell me," she told him. "Besides, it not like my Maggie won't tell me."

John nodded and then continued.

"Yesterday, Maggie and I engaged the attacking air and sub force. The attack was quite fierce, and we both sustained losses on our ends. The Aqua Marine's forces took quite a beating."

"Is Maggie alright?" Naomi said, her voice full of concern.

"Yes. She was a little rattled, but she's alright," John told her soothingly. Naomi visibly relaxed.

"Ricky, I need to know that we can really count on you," John said seriously. "You're very young to have this responsibility..."

"Don't worry about me!" Ricky said smiling. "Those tanks and I are unstoppable!"

Young and unstoppable, John thought. *As a new recruit always is.*

"So, we can count on you?" John said.

"Absolutely!" Ricky said confidently, giving his best smile.

Suddenly, Ricky's and John's M.A.D.'s went off. The colony's alarms could be heard outside in the hallways.

"The aliens are attacking again!" Isaac said over the communicator. "It's a new submarine force! Also, a ground force is approaching as well!"

"It's go time!" Ricky said. He grabbed his jacket and put it on.

John grabbed his shoulder.

"Ricky," he said to him quickly. "Maggie's subs are probably not fully repaired yet. Make sure you guard the ocean side. They could send forces to attack into the water."

"No sweat!" Ricky said.

Naomi had been watching his preparation intently. Ricky walked over to her and gave her a kiss.

"Leave it to me," Ricky told her.

Naomi smiled at him and nodded.

"Wish me luck!" he told them as he left, running to the M.A.D. Bunker.

We'll work on protocols, John thought.

"If you'll excuse me...oh!" John said startled. Naomi had gotten up and was dressing.

"No worries Captain," she said. She finally pulled her blouse on. John breathed deep.

She walked up to John "And you keep your mouth shut to Maggie, you hear me?" she told him fiercely. "What I do with my boyfriend is my business..."

Her eyes narrowed. "...as is what she does with you." she added.

John couldn't help but smile. *Just like Maggie*, he thought.

"John," Isaac said over the M.A.D. "They could both use a spotter on this one. Are you going to cover Ricky or Maggie?"

John thought to himself. *Of course, he would like to be close to Maggie, but he could not deny that Ricky needed guidance.*

"I'll join Ricky in the M.A.D. Bunker," John said. "You meet Maggie down in the M.A.D. Bay."

"Roger that!" Isaac said.

He left Naomi's and headed towards the M.A.D. Bunker.

"Maggie!" he said over the M.A.D Red. "Are you at the M.A.D. Bay?"

"Yes!" she said. "I heard about Ricky. You kept that boy in line out there, you hear?"

It'll be tough, John thought. And he ran off to the M.A.D. Bunker.

Chapter 23

John headed quickly down to the M.A.D. Bunker after Ricky. He finally caught up with him just before they reached the door.

"Ricky!" he yelled after him. Ricky turned around to look at him.

"Oh, hey Cap!" he said. "You here to give me a hand?"

John scowled.

"*Captain,*" John said to him sharply.

"Oh! Alright, Captain." Ricky corrected. "You're here to give me a hand?"

"Yes, I am," John told him. "I'll be at the console monitoring you this time. Keep your focus."

Ricky nodded to him, smiling.

They entered the bunker, and Ricky climbed up onto the boarding platform for the Dirt Driller. John sat down at the console and started up the monitoring systems.

***

Down in the M.A.D. Bay, Maggie was preparing to enter the Aqua Marine.

"Make sure to guard yourself well," Isaac told her from his seat at the console. "The mini-subs were heavily damaged in the last fight, and all the repairs haven't been completed yet. You're only at about half strength."

Maggie nodded to him. "I'll be alright." Then, she frowned. "Ricky will be handling things on the ground, then?"

"He will," Isaac said. Seeing her face, he added: "Hey really is a great guy underneath it all, you know."

Maggie grunted. "What my niece sees in him I'll never know." she said.

"Maggie!" they heard John say. "I'll be monitoring Ricky here, don't worry about him! You focus, alright?"

She smiled. *John will keep him in line*, she thought. She climbed onto the Aqua Marine and opened the hatch.

After activation, she submerged the Aqua Marine and had her mini-subs float out in front – her heart sank seeing how few she really had.

She could see the advancing enemy subs on her radar.

"Let's get started," she said to herself.

The torpedoes launched towards her, and she had her subs intercept as best she could, but the level of firepower coming at her was a lot more then she remembered from before.

"Hang in there Maggie!" Isaac yelled to her.

***

Ricky had just pulled his helmet onto his head. He heard John's voice.

"Ricky!" John barked at him. "Don't forget to guard the ocean side!"

"Don't worry, Captain!" Ricky replied cheerfully. "I got it!"

Ricky rolled out in his tanks. The approaching enemy ground force was already in sight.

"Wow," Ricky said in awe. "I guess there are a lot of them...aren't there?"

"Yes, I see them," John said to him. "Concentrate!"

"Oh no problem!" he replied. "Just more to blow up!"

John sighed.

***

Down in the waters, Maggie was surrounded by the sounds of explosions in the water. She was focusing all of her attention on the attacks being launched at her.

Isaac was tense as he watched the battle. *Could Maggie hold out?* He wondered. At least she was able to hold them at bay, but she did not have the force to hold off this kind of assault forever.

Finally, he watched as Maggie fired a shot through and impacted an enemy sub.

"Great shot!" Isaac yelled.

"Thanks, but I still have my hands full down here!" she yelled.

"I can see that!" Isaac said. "They don't appear to be advancing at all. Just keep up your current efforts, and I think you'll make it through this!"

***

Back in the M.A.D. Bunker, John could feel the rumbles and blasts outside of the colony as Ricky engaged the ground force.

John studied Ricky's form in his tanks. *All wrong*, he thought. *Ricky is more concerned with destroying tanks then he is with the colony's defense...though he is at least distracting the enemy with his fire.*

"Ricky!" he yelled to him. "You need to focus your attack patterns. Some of the attacks from the enemy are hitting the colony. You need to protect the wall of the colony!"

"On it, John!" Ricky said.

John let that one pass. He examined the screen carefully, noting Ricky current tank positions. Then, he saw something that jolted him.

"RICKY!" he yelled to him. "There are tanks approaching the ocean side. Get your tanks over and intercept them. We can't have them attacking Maggie from above!"

"Got it!" Ricky yelled.

John watched as Ricky directed his tanks towards the force moving towards the ocean.

Enemy tanks got in front of the Ricky's force as he approached.

"Hey!" John heard Ricky yell. "Get out of my way!"

Ricky fired upon the now blocking force. He was able to destroy that force fairly quickly, and he advanced.

Three tanks were advancing upon the ocean waters quickly. Ricky gave his orders to fire, and the lasers impacted two of them.

"One left!" Ricky said aloud, as he readied his final shot.

BOOM! Ricky watched as a tank he hadn't accounted for struck the Dirt Driller. The attack distracted his attention.

"Oh you son of a...," Ricky began.

"RICKY! THE OTHER TANK!" John yelled to him.

John switched his screen view quickly to see the sub battle were Maggie was holding out. Most of the enemy subs were gone, but the tank on the shore just barely showed up on the radar.

He watched a shot fire from it.

"MAGGIE!" John shouted.

Isaac saw the shot as well.

"MAGGIE!" he yelled. "ABOVE YOU!"

"AHHHHH!" they heard Maggie scream as the missile hit the top of the Aqua Marine.

"Maggie?!" Isaac yelled. "What happened?!" He watched on the screen as the Aqua Marine approached the M.A.D. Bay again.

MAGGIE! MAGGIE!" John yelled across the radio. He jumped up from his seat and dashed out of the M.A.D. Bunker and headed for the M.A.D. Bay as fast as he could.

    ***

In the Dirt Driller, Ricky was just finishing up with the remaining enemy tanks.

"Take that!" Ricky yelled, watching as the last of the enemy force exploded before him.

"Ah, finished!" he said to himself, pleased. "Hey, John, how did I do?"

He heard no answer.

"Oh sorry, *Captain*, how did I do?" he corrected.

Then, Isaac's voice came over the M.A.D. Black.

"Ricky!" he yelled. "Get down to the M.A.D. Bay! NOW!"

Chapter 24

John arrived in the M.A.D. Bay in panic.

"John!" Isaac said to him. "The Aqua Marine is surfacing!"

John and Isaac watched as the Aqua Marine surfaced in the M.A.D. Bay.

They both gasped.

Shattered metal and glass marked the hole at the front of the sub. They both saw Maggie's body under the water's surface, the area surrounded in blood.

Without a second thought, John dived into the water and got to Maggie's side. He pulled the broken helmet off her, and he pulled her to the surface. When he pulled her out of the water, he was shocked to see her faced horribly gashed with scars.

Isaac helped him get her to the ground of the bay. Her jumpsuit was torn down the side with gashes that had ripped the skin and bloodied her side.

"MAGGIE! MAGGIE!" John shouted in terror, shaking her.

Maggie did not respond.

John felt for a pulse on her neck, and he looked to her chest. No pulse, no breath.

"Get the medical team down here, NOW!" he roared at Isaac.

Isaac jumped at the order. "Y-yes sir!" he said, pulling out his communicator.

John unzipped her jacket and began CPR on her body.

"Come on Maggie!" he said, pushing into her chest in

rhythm. He applied the breaths to her mouth, and then repeated the chest motions.

"COME ON!" he wailed, his eyes welling up with tears.

Maggie coughed and gasped.

"Maggie!" John said in relief.

Her eyes saw him, and she smiled meekly.

"John...," she said, and she slowly and shakily brought up her hand to feel his cheek. "I...."

And then her arm fell to the floor, and her eyes lost focus.

"Ma...Maggie! MAGGIE!" John said, shaking her.

She did not respond.

At that moment, Ricky ran into the M.A.D. Bay. Before he said a word, a medical team arrived behind him led by Dr. Duncan.

"There!" Isaac yelled, pointing with his finger. "Dr. Cullen has been critically injured!"

Dr. Duncan's face paled. He began giving orders quickly to his medical staff. They swarmed in around Maggie, and John stood up and stepped back a few paces to give them room.

John and Isaac stood there tense for a few moments. Ricky stood silent and watched the proceedings from a distance – feeling uneasy.

Then, the medics spoke to Dr. Duncan. He grasped his face and breathed deeply.

He turned to John. "I'm sorry, Captain Rylund." Dr. Duncan said solemnly, tears in his eyes. "She's gone."

John's eyes welled with tears. He wiped his eyes with his sleeve, and he stared at Maggie's body. They all stepped away from her body at his gesture, and he got back down next to her. He took the necklace he made for her from around her neck and tucked it into his pocket.

And then he kissed her face.

He stood back up...and his eyes found Ricky standing in the M.A.D. Bay.

John walked over to him, his eyes full of fury – Ricky's face had paled.

He saw Ricky take a gulp.

He got in front of Ricky, staring down at him.

"Hey, J-John," he stammered. "I'm sorry about Mag..."

POW!

...and John fist impacted Ricky's face as hard as he could.

"YOU'RE FUCKING SORRY!" John roared, as Ricky's body fell to the floor.

"UUGGHHH!!" Ricky moaned, as he clenched his face.

John started to kick Ricky's body, wailing blows again his ribs with all the fury and passion in him. Ricky yelped in pain as he felt his ribs pounded by John's boots.

John heard cracking. He didn't care.

"CAPTAIN STOP!" Isaac yelled as he jumped in front of John with his hands up.

John breathed hard, looking down at Ricky's crying and moaning form. He barely had acknowledged Isaac.

He looked around. Dr. Duncan and his medics stared at him in shock.

He turned and walked out of the M.A.D. Bay, breathing hard and deep.

Isaac breathed a sigh of relief. *Thank god I stopped him,* he thought.

Dr. Duncan watched John go, and his eyes gave a brief glint of triumph.

"Tend to Ricky," Isaac said.

Dr. Duncan shook himself back to the present and turned to Isaac.

"Bring him to the infirmary," Isaac added, "and bring Maggie's body there as well."

Dr. Duncan nodded and gave instructions to his medics who began their work.

Isaac got on his communicator. "Get me the Agro sector. Naomi Reins please."

Chapter 25

Naomi sat crying in the infirmary next to the body of her aunt.

She just could not believe that Maggie was dead. Isaac had contacted her and told her to come to the infirmary. She had assumed that Maggie was simply injured...but this...

She started moaning again. She hadn't been able to stop.

Isaac came and sat down next to her. He put his arm around her.

"Naomi," he said to her gently. "I'm so sorry..."

Naomi kept sobbing. She barely acknowledged him. Isaac just sat there, saying nothing.

"Where's Ricky?" Naomi said, as she wiped her eyes.

Isaac paused. Ricky was laying in one of the rooms of the infirmary. Naomi hadn't seen him being brought in.

"Um...," Isaac said nervously.

"Oh no!" she wailed, turning her eyes towards him. "NOT HIM TOO!!"

"No! Ricky's alive!" Isaac assured her. He pointed down the hall and said: "He's down that way!"

Naomi picked herself up and hurried down the infirmary hallway, looking into each room to see if Ricky was there.

Finally, she found his room, and she rushed in and put her arms around him. His face was heavily bruised on one side, and his ribs were wrapped in bandages.

"Oh my god, Ricky!" Naomi said to him, caressing his face.

He had been resting. He roused himself, and groaned. His eyes met Naomi's.

"Oh...hey Naomi," he said weakly. "AH! My head!"

Naomi examined his face. The bruise on his face was black and blue. She touched it, and he winced.

"Ouch! Easy, that hurts!" he moaned.

"Sorry!" she said. "You must have taken a pretty bad hit out there!"

Ricky said nothing. His eyes were watering.

"Oh, I'm sorry!" she said to him, her voice choking.

"You're sorry?" he said, starting to cry. "Maggie's dead..."

"I know!" she said, starting to cry.

Naomi stood there next to Ricky sobbing for several minutes.

When she calmed herself enough, she noticed Ricky giving her a look.

"I could have saved her," he said simply, tears in his eyes. "I could have saved her...but I couldn't..."

Naomi paused, taking in what he had said. She wiped her eyes. "This wasn't your fault, Ricky!" she told him fiercely. "Do you hear me! NOT YOU'RE FAULT!"

Ricky turned away, wincing as his ribs ached. "If I had protected the ocean side as I was told by John," he said in bitter voice. "Maggie would still be here..."

He turned back to Naomi (wincing yet again). His face was tense and he shouted: "YOUR AUNT WOULD STILL BE ALIVE IF IT WASN'T FOR ME! AH!"

Ricky grabbed at his ribs, moaning. He slowly turned away again. Naomi could hear his weeping.

"You were trying to defend the colony!" Naomi countered. "It's not John's fault you had your hands full. Look at you! You got injured too!"

Ricky turned slowly back to her. "I didn't get these injuries from the battle with the aliens," he said evenly.

Naomi was puzzled. "Wait...then why are you all banged up?"

***

121

Naomi charged out of Ricky's room and marched down the hallway. Dr. Duncan was walking the other way as she approached.

"Ms. Reins," he said gravely, "I am sorry about...HEY!"

Naomi shoved him aside as she strode down the hallway.

Dr. Duncan stumbled and nearly fell. He recovered and straightened his coat.

Excuse me, he said to himself. *At least I give a damn.*

***

John was sitting in his quarters. He sat on his bed, staring at the fishing lure necklace he had taken from Maggie's body, his eyes red from tears.

His mind was racing with the events of the past hour.

I can't believe I lost control like that, he thought. *But...Maggie...I can't believe she's gone.*

He could still see her face, her hair...

Suddenly, there was a loud knock on his door.

"JOHN!" he heard a voice shout, "OPEN THIS DAMN DOOR!"

I know that voice, he thought.

He stood up and walked over. Opening the door, he saw Naomi there.

She stepped boldly into his room as he stepped back. She slammed the door behind her.

"WHO THE HELL DO YOU THINK YOU ARE BEATING THE SHIT OUT OF RICKY?!" she roared at him.

John was affronted.

"That little boy is the reason Maggie's dead!" he said to her sternly.

"Maggie's dead because aliens attacked our planet!" she countered. "Unless you forgot that?!"

"HE DISOBEYED MY ORDERS!" John roared at her, getting angry again. "I AM THE CAPTAIN OF THIS COLONY!"

"SO THE CAPTAIN HAS THE RIGHT TO BEAT THE CRAP OUT OF PEOPLE HE DOESN'T LIKE!?" she yelled to him, her eyes in tears.

On impulse, John shoved Naomi. She slammed into the closed door.

122

"I'VE HAD ENOUGH OF YOUR PESTERING, GIRL!" he shouted at her.

Naomi stood against the door, trembling. She looked at John with a mixture of hatred and fear. Tears dripped down her face.

John blinked. He looked in her eyes and saw the pain.

He also saw how her eyes were just like Maggie's....and Evelyn's....

He stared at his hands. *What have I done?* He thought.

He looked back up at her. Weeping, Naomi opened the door and ran down the hall.

John sat himself down on his bed, staring at his hands.

What have I done?

And, he began to sob again. *What have I done?*

Chapter 26

Ricky lay still in the infirmary bed.

It was his fault he thought, tears in his eyes.

John told him to guard the ocean side. But he just had to have his fun. He had to blow up the tanks. It was all so fun...

Fun. He thought. *Was that all he wanted?*

But...that's all he had...since...

He closed his eyes...remembering...

His friends had asked him to come out of town for a party. He had been bored for a few days now, and he really wanted some excitement.

He was packing an overnight bag, when his dad came down the hall and saw what he was doing.

"And just where are you going?" he asked him, raising an eyebrow.

Ricky turned and looked up, smiling as he always did.

"Oh, hey pop! Some of the guys are getting a party together out of town," he told him. "I'll be gone for a few nights."

Ricky's father rolled his eyes.

"Another party?" he told him. "Don't you think it's time you got a job?"

Ricky shuddered. *This argument again?*

"Dad," he told him, as he tucked some CDs into his duffel bag. "You always rat on me about that..."

"I WILL RAT ON YOU AS LONG AS IT TAKES, BOY!"

he scolded. "When are you gonna grow up and get your ass up and out of this house, Ricky!?"

Ricky was offended.

"What?" he said to his father. "I thought you liked having my company around the house – now that Pete and Claire are off at college."

"Yes, *off at college*," he said deliberately. "At least they have made some choices and are doing something with their lives!"

Ricky stopped his packing. He sat down on his bed.

"I don't know what to tell you dad," he said. "I've never been smart, so I was never going to college. I barely squeaked by high school."

"There was always the military," his father offered.

"Me?" Ricky said. "You're kidding, right? I wouldn't last five seconds on the battlefield!"

"Tell that to your gaming buddies in that shooting game you play together," his dad retorted.

"That's different," he said.

"OH, DAMN YOU RICKY!" he said, losing her temper. "You can't 'hang around' forever! Enjoy your partying, but you better have some plan for your ass when you get back!"

And with that, he stormed out.

Ricky rolled his eyes. *He'll never understand me*, he thought.

An hour later, with his guitar in hand, Ricky's friends had picked him up, and they traveled out of town. The party had been quite a smash: loud music, alcohol, girls – everything he liked.

While the party was approaching the late hours, there were suddenly some loud explosions in the night. The music was turned off. People walked outside...

...and everyone gasped as they saw the alien crafts flying through the sky, blowing up the buildings with their laser beams.

People screamed and ran.

In all the confusion, Ricky had managed to grab his duffel bag and his guitar. He found someone's car keys that he recognized, but he couldn't find the person. His mind had gone to one thought – was his dad alright?

He drove the car down the road, thankfully he never ran into any of the attacking alien craft – though he did see many of them on the horizon. He turned on the radio, and he heard the announcement of alien attacks. The announcer asked people to be calm and head to safe zones in their communities.

Ricky drove the car home as fast as he could. He would get his dad. Then, maybe they could meet up with his siblings at...

...he rolled down his street, and he moaned in agony.

His home had been destroyed. He walked through the rubble, looking for any sign of his father.

He found his body under some fallen boards – charred and bloodied. He moaned and cried.

"It's all my fault," he said aloud as he lay in the bed. "He's dead because of me...and Maggie's dead because of me..."

He cried and moaned. *If I had been there*, he thought, *they would both still be alive. I could have saved them from the aliens....*

...the aliens...

He stopped crying. He stopped moaning.

The aliens.

He looked at the table next to him. His gray jacket and his M.A.D. Black lay there.

He picked up the M.A.D. Black. *His* M.A.D. Black.

The alarms sounded off in the colony corridors...his M.A.D. Black buzzed.

Now was the time to do something.

Chapter 27

Naomi was in her quarters. She was sitting on her bed looking at her locket – her father's picture staring at her.

Her eyes were welled up with tears. She wiped her eyes with her sleeve. She hated John for hurting Ricky, and she hated how he'd shoved her.

She hated being shoved.

The boy in middle school had shoved her into the lockers.

"Oh, tough new girl needs to be taught a lesson!" the boy jeered. "Doesn't she boys?"

It was her first week at her new school after her father had died. Naomi had been so upset over the loss of her dad that she simply hadn't been paying attention to anyone. She had walked right by this boy while holding her locket in her hands.

The boy didn't appreciate being ignored.

He walked up to her now, cracking his knuckles. Naomi stood her ground. Her eyes stared at the boy.

"What's that?" he said, snatching the locket from Naomi's hand.

"Give that back!" Naomi said fiercely. No one messed with her locket – or her father.

"And what are you gonna do if I don't?" he laughed. "I don't like *girls* telling me what to do!"

Before he knew what happened, Naomi had punched him in the gut as hard as she could. She grabbed the locket from his hand

and elbowed him across the face. He fell to the ground, crying.

Two other boys nearby stood stunned. They had never seen anyone take out the school bully.

"Either of you two want some? THEN BACK OFF!" she roared.

The boys ran off.

A teacher had noticed the fight, and Naomi was sent home for the day. She walked home crying and ran to her room. Maggie had the day off and was startled by Naomi's sudden appearance.

"Naomi?" Maggie said, hearing her cry. She ran after her to her bedroom.

Maggie saw Naomi crying on her bed. She came in and sat down next to her niece.

"Naomi, tell me what happened," Maggie said to her.

After wiping her tears away, Naomi told her aunt what had happened at school. Maggie listened intently.

After she finished, Naomi looked up at her aunt. Maggie was smiling at her.

"Your father would be so proud of you," Maggie told her simply.

Naomi lifted herself up and hugged her aunt.

"You can't be beating up boys in school," Maggie told her firmly.

Naomi nodded.

"Not all boys treat girls like that," Maggie assured her. "Some will be a bit rough around the edges..."

"...like Dr. Duncan?" Naomi chimed in, smirking.

Maggie shuddered. "Yes," she said crisply. "like Dr. Duncan."

They both laughed.

"I know how much you miss your father," Maggie said solemnly. "I miss him too."

Naomi said nothing.

"Someday, you won't feel like you do right now," she told her. "It will take time, but someday, it will feel better."

Maggie stood up and left Naomi sitting on her bed.

Naomi pulled out her father's locket and held it close to her.

He would never have treated her badly. He was always fun. He loved her...

...these boys would never love her the same way, she thought. *No boy ever would.* So, she never let a boy get close. She just felt that, in some way, they would never hold up to her father. Boys at that age want a girlfriend, naturally, but, they just wanted to make out or have bragging rights to their friends.

Boys approached her during those years, but she brushed them off...or fought them off. She gained a reputation for a fierce personality and will.

And that's how it had been for the past five years...

Until she met Ricky...

When the alien attacks started, Dr. Duncan had contacted Maggie, and he told her about the colony of Terra. They could find refuge. Maggie had brought along Naomi, naturally, and, after some tense days, they all arrived at the Terra colony gates.

After being led inside, they all had lined up for registration.

"Hey, you drop this?" the man called from behind her. Naomi looked behind her and saw a tall young man wearing denim jeans and a faded jacket holding her locket. She checked her neck quickly and realized that the clasp must have broken without her noticing. He walked over and handed the locket to her.

"Thanks," Naomi said to him, her cheeks flushing. "My name's Naomi."

The young man stood at his full height and held out his hand.

"I'm Ricky Plik," he told her, his cheeks flushing. "It's nice to meet you."

Naomi smiled at him, and he smiled back.

"Can I carry your bags?" he offered, as he took them from her. Naomi made no move to stop him.

Maggie had turned around in line when she realized that Naomi was no longer behind her.

"Nao...Naomi! Come on!" she called to her.

Naomi stepped up with Ricky following. Maggie peered at him curiously.

"OH!" Naomi said quickly, realizing the need for introduction. "Maggie, this is Ricky! Ricky, this is my aunt, Dr. Maggie Cullen."

"Hey Mags!" Ricky said cheerfully, holding out his hand.

Maggie scowled. "Pleasure," she said evenly, shaking his hand.

After that, Naomi had found herself spending a lot of time with Ricky. It was so strange not to just reject him. She just felt...comfortably with him. She just kept thinking back to when she met him...and he brought her locket back to her...

...and how her aunt had taken to him. *She never did like him,* Naomi thought to herself

But now, Maggie was gone.

She cried. *How long had it been since she cried this much?*

"IT'S NOT FAIR!" she yelled out.

Now there was no one to hear her. No one to comfort her. No one to hold her...

...no one except Ricky.

And I'll be damned if I'm gonna let anything more happen to him...

She picked herself up, and, putting her locket around her neck, she walked back to the infirmary to see Ricky.

Chapter 28

John sat weeping in his quarters.

It was all Ricky's fault, he thought. *He wasn't there for her...*
Why did he choose to spot for Ricky and not her? She would
still be here if not for me! He told himself angrily.

...and his eyes fell on the gold band on his finger...

I wasn't there for her...

When the alien attacks had begun, John and Evelyn were
living on base. Cities had been leveled quickly, and John had been
called on to take action along with his unit.

"You're going?" Evelyn asked him, her eyes full of worry.

John was busy getting dressed in combat gear.

"I have to Evelyn," he told her seriously. "The alien attacks
are increasing daily. My unit and I have been called up to help."

Evelyn sat down on their bed. She started weeping.

"Evelyn," John said, as he walked over and sat down next to
her. He kissed her gently and hugged her.

"E-Everything is happening so fast...," she stuttered.
"What's....what's going to happen to us all?"

John sat silent. "I don't know," he eventually told her. "But, I
promise I will come back for you. I will keep us safe."

Evelyn's eyes watered with tears. He brushed a tear away
with his finger.

"Just stay here till I get back," he told her. "It's the safest
place for you right now."

At that moment, there was a knock their door. John walked out of the bedroom, down the stairs, and to the front door. Evelyn followed after him.

Joseph Hall stood there in full uniform. They saluted each other.

"Are you ready, John?" he asked him.

John turned around, and Evelyn jumped into his arms. John kissed her again. They brought their hands up and looked at their wedding bands.

It's only been three years, he thought. *Please, let us have more.*

He then turned and left. Evelyn watched him enter the transport – him giving her a farewell wave as he went. She watched the transport drive away until it was out of sight.

John and Joseph were both sent to do recon and report back on the movement patterns of the alien attacks. They both flew off together, and, in a few hours, did locate the aliens attacking yet another city.

As soon as they did, they received distress signals coming from their base, and they flew back.

Upon arriving, they found that their base had been attacked by the aliens shortly after their departure. Fear had gripped John's heart as he saw the smoking remains of the residences. People lay dead all around. Upon using their radios, they were unable to get any response from the command centers.

"THEY'RE ALL DEAD! EVERY LAST ONE OF THEM!" Joseph yelled to John over the radio.

John and Joseph landed on what remained of the base's runway, and they went off in search of survivors.

John ran down the road and came to his house.

He found his home mostly intact, and the door was ajar.

"EVELYN!" he called as he ran inside.

As he stepped into the house further, he heard a groaning sound. He turned a corner and found Evelyn lying on the hallway floor.

He ran over to her, his heart lifting at her sight. *She's alive!* He thought.

"EVELYN!" he said, turning her over.

He gasped and his heart sank.

Her face was covered in bloody cuts, and her left arm hung limply. Blood covered the floor.

She opened her eyes meekly.

"John...," she said, her voice trembling.

"I'm here!" he said, holding her good hand with his. "Don't worry...I'll get help..."

"He came...," she said, and then she passed out.

"Who came? EVELYN!" he said, shaking her body.

He felt her neck. No pulse. The blood on the floor told him she was beyond hope.

Then, he heard noises upstairs that sounded like someone. Anger and pain fueling him, he ran up the stairs.

He found a young man in their bedroom rummaging through the closets and wardrobes. Money, jewelry, and other valuables were tossed on the bed – a bloody knife lay nearby.

"YOU FUCKING LITTLE!" John shouted as he ambushed the man. He landed a good solid punch across his face.

The man fell to the floor, crying and moaning.

John began whaling punches on his body, hammering him over and over again.

After a few minutes of this, John stepped back...the man was barely conscious. He stared at John...

"What d-does...it m-matter, bro?" he said weakly. "It's end times...n-none of us are gonna make it..."

He then passed out and died on the floor.

"JOHN!" John heard a voice yell from the doorway. Joseph stood there. "I FOUND EVELYN'S BODY IN THE HALL! WHAT'S GOING..."

John had fallen to his knees sobbing – he had never cried harder in his life.

This stupid kid killed Evelyn. This stupid kid came in and killed her...and he couldn't stop him.

It was his fault. It was his fault she was gone. He should have been there for her.

The aliens caused this all to happen, he thought to himself. *Regardless of Ricky's abilities or actions, the aliens are ultimately what caused this to happen. Just like Naomi said...*

Naomi!

He looked at his hands. He remembered her eyes, how

frightened they looked.

He stood up. *I have to find her.*

Chapter 29

Dr. Torre sat in his laboratory, pondering over recent events. On his screen, he monitored the repairs of the Dirt Driller and the Aqua Marine...

The Aqua Marine...

The death of Dr. Maggie Cullen weighed heavily on his mind. The M.A.D. Blue, the Aqua Marine's control device, sat on his desk (it had been recovered, undamaged). With the D.N.A. Lock, Dr. Torre had safeguarded the technology from being used by anyone other than the first person who touched it. Now that Maggie was gone...

"DAMN IT ALL!" Isaac shouted out loud. He slammed his hand down on his desk in frustration.

He had been going over the code on his screen for hours now. There was no getting around it.

I can't change the original designation code, he thought to himself. *Maggie touched it first, so she's the only person who can use it. Damn it! Damn it! DAMN IT!*

If another ocean attack happened, they would be finished.

He leaned back in his chair. Aliens attacking. Humanity dying. What got him here?

Well, with any good origin story, he thought, *you start at the beginning...*

The orphanage.

The people there had raised him since he was a baby. No one knew who his parents or family were.

What they did know was that he was smart.

It wasn't every kid who could do algebra in grade school. His teachers had noticed his amazing skills, and he had gone to some of the finest private schools to help his talent develop.

As a result, he had finished high school by 16, completed his science and engineering degree at 20, and his doctorate at 24. He was one of the youngest scientists working in the world.

And yet, he had to admit he was incredibly lonely.

When you are that smart, most 'normal' kids don't spend time with you, or you have so much practice and study to do you don't have time for them. As a result, he didn't have many friends growing up.

Hell, he didn't have any friends growing up.

Compound that with not having family...and you wind up pretty lonely.

As a result, Isaac spent most of his time with comic books – one of his only hobbies. He had learned most of those plot lines and stories by heart. His collections were expansive.

And, you know what? That was all he really cared about. Yeah, he could do the equations. He could design, he could build, and he could work out complex problems. But, he never felt he did anything 'real' with what he did.

Now, *superheroes*? They did things. They affected the world. They saved lives. They were important.

When the aliens starting attacking the planet, he wondered where the heroes were. This is just when heroes should come and save them all...

...and then the phone rang at his apartment. He picked it up.

"Hello?" he said curiously.

"Is this Dr. Isaac Torre?" a man's voice asked.

"Yes it is," Isaac replied.

"Dr. Torre, my name is Captain Glenn Orvis," he said firmly. "I am the head of a colony called Terra, which we are establishing as a safe haven for whatever population we can gather and protect. We need talent to help design defenses for the colony against the alien invaders. Are you interested?"

Are you kidding? Isaac thought excitedly. *They need my*

genius to help save and protect humanity? A brilliant scientist like me was going to be the hero and figure out how to stop them? Sign me up!

So, he gathered up his notebooks and computers, as well as his action figures, toys, and comics. And, with the directions he had been given, headed towards the colony of Terra – the last safe haven for humanity.

The trip had been mostly one of thinking – and dodging flights of alien crafts. He drove down the road thinking to himself: *What could the colony possibly ask him to do? Would he have to design weapons? Would have to make a suit or machine that could defend humanity? Would there be super powers? Would there be...*

"AHHH!" he shouted as he slammed on the brakes.

There was a car broken down in the lane of travel. A young man stood in front of the open hood. Smoke poured out of the engine.

Isaac pulled to the side. He stepped out. He wasn't much of a mechanic, but he'd see what he could do.

"Hey," he said to the guy. "Can I help?"

The young man looked up at him. "I don't think anything is gonna help this out!" he moaned. "DAMN IT!"

This guy is upset, Isaac noted.

"Where are you heading?" he asked him.

"I DON'T KNOW!" he said, moaning. He sat himself down on the road and started weeping.

Huh. Awkward, Isaac thought.

He went and sat down next to the guy. It just felt like the right thing to do.

"Hey," Isaac said. "There no need to cry. It'll be alright..."

"WHAT'S GONNA BE ALRIGHT?!" the man yelled at him.

Isaac couldn't figure out what to say to him. He just kept sitting there crying.

"I-I don't h-have a place to go...," he said through his tears.

Isaac hadn't considered if he ran into anyone on the way to Terra. What with all the alien attacks, people were panicking worldwide...

...but Terra would be taking in refugees.

"Hey," Isaac said. "I'm heading to a safe place from the alien attacks. Would you like to come with me and join up?"

The man's eyes glinted with hope.

"Sure," he said meekly. "Let me get my stuff from the car..."

He slowly got himself up and open his car door. The man retrieved a duffel bag and a guitar from the backseat.

"Hmm, is that it?" Isaac said. He would have thought, given the current circumstances, that the guy would have had more with him.

"Yeah," he said. "That's all. Why?"

Isaac said nothing but gestured for the man to hop in his car.

Isaac got back in his driver's seat and, after tossing his guitar and duffel bag in the back seat, the man took shotgun beside him.

"I'm Isaac, but the way. Isaac Torre," Isaac said to him, offering his hand. Isaac hated the formality of being called 'doctor', so he never bothered to mention it when meeting someone.

"Well, I'm Ricky. Ricky Plik," the man replied, shaking his hand.

"So," Ricky asked him, raising an eyebrow towards the backseat, "what's with all the comic books?"

Isaac scowled at him...and it wouldn't be the only time that trip he did so.

And that was how Isaac began his friendship with Ricky. He never had someone that close to talk with before. Ricky wasn't a smart man compared to Isaac – or a rock, frankly – though he was witty and easy-going. Isaac found out he was into music and just enjoyed having fun. He felt they complimented each other quite well.

Our road trip would make a good story to write down sometime, Isaac thought to himself.

And, eventually, Isaac and Ricky made it to Terra.

They made their way to the registration line. While waiting, Isaac noticed Ricky staring at something.

He tapped Ricky on the shoulder.

"Uh, Ricky," he said. "Are you OK?"

"Wow," Ricky said softly. "She's beautiful."

Isaac followed his line of sight and noticed a young blonde girl standing in one of the other lines.

Ricky dropped his guitar and duffel bag and ran over to her. Isaac watched as he bent down and grabbed a locket on the ground just behind the young woman. He watched as Ricky presented it to her.

"Excuse me," a voice said behind him. "Are you Dr. Isaac Torre?"

Isaac turned around and saw the tall, gray-haired man standing behind him.

"I'm Captain Glenn Orvis," he said, extending his hand.

And with that, Isaac was taken into the inner circle of confidence in the colony. It was then that he began developing the M.A.D. Technology...

Now this is what life should be about! He just thought: *Everyone is counting on the brilliant scientist Dr. Isaac Torre to save humanity from destruction! The aliens stood no chance against his genius and cunning. He would create a team of heroes that would band together and....*

"DAMN IT!" he yelled in frustration again. "If only I could get around my own damn D.N.A. lock I put in this thing!" He grabbed the M.A.D. Blue and shook it in his hand.

But no! He had to make it perfect! He had to make his coding flawless! Infallible!

Now that Maggie was dead...his flawlessness and infallibility could doom them all!

At that moment, the alarms went off.

Damn it, Isaac thought, tucking the M.A.D. Blue into his pocket. *Please let it not be an ocean attack. And, even if it isn't, how will John and Ricky to work together now?*

***

John was heading towards Naomi's quarters when alarms started going off in hallways and his M.A.D. Red buzzed.

"Captain Rylund!" Isaac said over the M.A.D. Red. "The aliens are attacking again! It's an air and ground assault!"

"I'll head to the M.A.D. Hangar!" he said without hesitation.

"Are you sure you're able, Captain?" Isaac asked him.

John sighed. *I'll talk to Naomi later,* he thought.

"It's my duty to the colony," John said gravely.

Back in his lab, Isaac pondered contacting Ricky. *Was he in a condition to fight?*

Chapter 30

Alarms blared around Ricky in the infirmary. Grabbing his M.A.D. Black off the stand, he slowly got himself up, his ribs wincing in pain as he did so.

I have to do this, he thought to himself, as he pulled his jacket on.

"Ricky!" Isaac yelled over the M.A.D. Black. "Are you there?"

"Yes, Isaac!" Ricky said firmly. "I'm here..."

"There's a ground force coming towards the colony, as well as an air force," he told Ricky hurriedly. "John is already heading to the M.A.D. Hangar. I know you're injured..."

"YOU'RE DAMN RIGHT HE IS!" a voice yelled from the doorway.

Dr. Duncan stood there.

"You are not going anywhere in your condition!" Dr. Duncan said fiercely. "I forbid it!"

Ricky stood up from his bed slowly, his ribs wincing in pain as he did so. Dr. Duncan entered the room and strode up to him. Ricky stood at his full height and stared at Dr. Duncan. He brought the M.A.D. Black to his face to speak to Isaac.

"I'm going, Isaac," he said simply. "If I don't, we'll all die." Ricky retorted, his voice pained as he started walking out of the infirmary, his ribs aching.

Neither Isaac nor Dr. Duncan could believe what they were

hearing.

"What's the status of my tanks?" Ricky said as he walked out of the room.

Isaac jumped out of his shock. "Y-You're at less than 40% capacity right now," Isaac said.

Ricky moaned softly as he walked. *Oh, that's not good*, he thought.

Dr. Duncan stepped out of the doorway and yelled down to Ricky: "YOU REALIZE YOU'RE GOING TO FIGHT ALONG SIDE THE MAN WHO NEARLY KILLED YOU!?"

Ricky kept walking. *I probably would have tried to kill me too*, Ricky thought to himself. He walked out of the infirmary and headed down the hallway. People were running around him, heading towards the security barracks.

"I'm coming to the M.A.D. Bunker as fast as I can," Ricky said to Isaac over his M.A.D. Black.

"You're WHAT?!" he heard a voice say ahead him.

Naomi ran up to him and held him.

"You can't be serious!" she told him in a panic. "Your injuries..."

Ricky walked deliberately out of her hands, and he continued towards the bunker, wincing every few moments.

"RICKY!" she shouted at him. She walked up ahead of him to attempt to bar his way.

He stopped and looked at her square in the eye.

"I'm going," he told her firmly. "Come if you want."

Naomi was stunned. She had never heard him speak like this.

Ricky brought his M.A.D. Black up to his face. "Isaac, I could use a spotter given my condition."

"You got it!" Isaac said. Then, Naomi and Ricky heard Isaac say: "Captain, are you going to be alright in the air without support?"

In the M.A.D. Hangar, John was climbing into the Fire Flyer. "You keep an eye on Ricky, Isaac" John said firmly.

Ricky nodded. Naomi was lost for words.

Naomi put her shoulder under Ricky's arm to help support him, and together, they walked towards the M.A.D. Bunker. People running past Ricky and Naomi looked upon him with concern.

141

Ricky soon arrived at the bunker with Naomi.

Isaac turned in the console chair. He was stunned seeing Naomi there. "What is she doing..."

"He needed help getting here!" Naomi protested. Isaac didn't comment further.

"You sure about this?" Isaac said to him.

"Positive," Ricky said without hesitation.

He started walking towards the Dirt Driller platform.

"Wait!" Naomi said. Ricky turned to her.

She cupped his face with her hands and kissed him on the lips.

"Be careful," she said softly to him.

He nodded to her.

Ricky walked up the platform, the sound of his occasionally moan of pain echoed in the room.

Both Isaac and Naomi watched him – Naomi in admiration and Isaac in disbelief.

Ricky got to the door and entered, and he climbed into the seat.

"Ouch," he winced, as he sat back, placing the M.A.D. Black in the console. He pulled the helmet down on his head.

"John is already engaging the air assault." Isaac said in his ear. "The ground forces are approaching fast."

Ricky had the Dirt Driller start up. The rumble made him wince. His ribs were throbbing.

I can do this, he told himself.

He had the other tanks start up as the bunker door opened up.

The Dirt Driller rolled forward, and his screen showed the enemy approaching. With each bump and rock of the tank, he moaned and grunted from the pain in his ribs.

This is gonna be rough, he thought.

He had the tanks fire on the enemy. The explosions rocked the space about him.

The force of tanks attacking the colony fired shot after shot, some of his tanks flipped and exploded about him. He had his tanks protect the border of the colony. He didn't really have the force to assault them head on.

Damn it, Ricky thought. This is the best I can do. *I hope John's holding up better than I am.*

***

Up in the air, John was dealing with the impressive onslaught of alien fighters.

He was using every flight skill he knew. His jets were getting blown from the sky left and right. He was tense with concentration.

I'm doing this for everyone, he thought. *Evelyn. Maggie. I will get through this.*

***

Down in the M.A.D. Bunker, Isaac and Naomi were viewing the radar screens in the air and the ground.

"They're getting creamed out there!" Naomi panicked.

"I know!" Isaac said. He had engaged the gun turrets on the sides of the colony. They were helping to take some of the aliens down, but it was barely scratching this onslaught.

Naomi looked at the radar of Ricky's tank battle. He was getting slammed hard.

Ricky is that tank out there, she thought. *In pain with every movement, but fighting. Fighting to save us all. And me...*

"If only we had more firepower!" Isaac yelled. He took the M.A.D. Blue from out of his pocket and shook it once more in frustration. "Not as if the Aqua Marine could help us!"

He slammed the device down on the desk.

Naomi looked at it curiously. *That's what Maggie was using to pilot the Aqua Marine*, she thought.

Maggie. Her eyes teared up again. *Maggie was dead. She was in it when the tanks blasted her...*

"Isaac," Naomi said suddenly, wiping her eyes. "I want to pilot the Aqua Marine."

He turned in surprise to her.

"I'm not letting Ricky die out there!" she said through tears. Then, steeling herself, she added: "I want to help!"

She explained the plan that she had thought of. He frowned.

"Great idea," he said. "But, as you probably know, the

M.A.D. Blue only works for the person who touches it first," he said, having had this frustration in his head for hours now. "And since Maggie touched it first, her D.N.A..."

"I'M HER NIECE!" Naomi shouted at him. "DOESN'T THAT COUNT FOR SOMETHING?!"

Isaac froze. He had completely forgotten about that. His mind raced mentally through the code he had written only weeks ago. *When I wrote the code, did I...*

"OH, DAMN YOU! JUST GIVE IT TO ME!" Naomi yelled in frustration, as she reached out and grabbed the M.A.D. Blue.

For a moment, nothing happened. Then, the screen turned on, and sounds buzzed and clicked. Then, the screen showed the words: Naomi Reins: M.A.D. Blue – Aqua Marine Pilot.

"GO!" Isaac shouted, and Naomi ran for the M.A.D. Bay.

Chapter 31

Isaac watched Naomi head out towards the M.A.D. Bay.
Why didn't I think of that? He thought.

He spun around in his chair and refocused on the battle.

"JOHN! RICKY!" Isaac yelled over the radio. "Are you holding up alright!?"

"Ugh...," he heard Ricky grunt. "I'm trying my best here!"

"I'm not fairing much better!" John shouted. "GET OFF MY TAIL!"

Isaac turned his attention back to the console.

Many of John's mini jets had been blown from the sky. Ricky wasn't fairing any better on the ground – his tanks barely holding off the attacks to the colony. Isaac could hear explosions against the colony walls.

Hurry, Naomi. Isaac thought. *They need help.*

***

John had not only been concentrating on his battle in the air, but he had been observing the fight on the ground from his view screen.

That kid has real guts, he thought to himself. *He's in pain and agony, but he's still fighting.*

...and its pain that I caused, he reminded himself.

"Ricky," John said. "Can you hear me?"

"Yes," Ricky said. "What it is, Captain?"

"I wanted to say I'm sorry," John said, his voice still tense, but with a hint of weariness. "When Maggie died...I just..."

"I know," Ricky said, grasping his ribs, the sounds of explosions filled the air around him. "And I know I could have done better."

John smiled. Then, an explosion on the tail side rattled him back to the battle.

"I'M HIT HARD!" John yelled. Some mini jets came to repair the Fire Flyer, leaving him short on aircraft.

"JOHN!" Ricky yelled.

Then, the Dirt Driller got impacted hard by enemy fire.

"RICKY!" Isaac yelled.

Suddenly, Ricky watched as a missile of some type impacted an enemy tank nearby.

"What the...," Ricky said in shock.

He checked his radar. He watched as more of the shots were coming from...

...the ocean?

Torpedoes fired from the ocean and slammed into the enemy tanks with unerring accuracy.

"ARE YOU OK, RICKY?!" he heard a voice shout in his ear.

Naomi!? Ricky realized, his mind racing.

The enemy tanks were too preoccupied dodging the new assault. They scattered to get away. Many exploded.

"Fire into the air, Ricky!" Naomi shouted. "HELP OUT JOHN!"

Ricky had his remaining tanks angle their fire into the air. The drill lasers shot into the air and collided with the flying aircraft.

John had been dodging the enemy when the drill beams come up from the ground.

"JOHN, YOU ALRIGHT?!" Ricky yelled to him.

John had to recover himself from the appearance of fire that came from below.

Barely, he thought. *I hardly have any jets left.*

"I'm fine!" John said. "Thanks for the assist!"

"I'm not the one you should thank," Ricky said. "But there will be time for that later. Get yourself clear of the fire!"

John flew himself out of the crossfire and looked at his radar.

The enemy aircraft were falling from the sky to Ricky's onslaught. He switched the radar view, and he saw that Ricky's ground enemy was gone.

How did that happen? He thought to himself. Due to the static and noise of explosions, he had not heard what had transpired in the M.A.D. Bunker earlier.

In a few short moments, the enemy air craft remaining had flown away from the colony. The damaged aircraft had fallen from the sky and crashed into the ground.

"Damn, that was a close one," Ricky said to no one in particular. He was still clutching his ribs.

***

Naomi stepped out of the hatch of the Aqua Marine. She wasn't sure how she felt.

She had wanted to help to save Ricky from getting killed. But, sitting in the place where Maggie had gotten killed was a little unnerving. She felt nauseous and her body was shaking.

The black space all around her had felt so...claustrophobic. How frightening it must have been for Maggie – to hear the explosion above her, to have water rush in all around her...

...to drown alone.

Naomi shook her head. She had to focus. She looked at the M.A.D. Blue in her hand.

"I did it, Maggie," she said with tears in her eyes. "I did it."

She was about to leave when she spotted something over on the side of the M.A.D. Bay.

"Might as well," she said.

***

Ricky drove the Dirt Driller and his remaining tanks back to the M.A.D. Bunker. He got himself out the tank, groaning at the pain in his ribs.

Isaac stood up from the console and ran up the platform. He helped steady Ricky as he walked.

"You crazy fool!" Isaac said to him. "I can't believe you did that."

"I didn't have...AH!...a choice." Ricky said with a groan.

Isaac helped him down the platform and walked him to his chair at the console.

At that moment, Naomi ran into the M.A.D. Bunker – wearing a gray M.A.D. jumpsuit with blue stripes.

"RICKY!" she said, running over to him.

"Hey, Naomi...," he said to her, giving his broadest smile. "You did great! Hey, where did you get that jumpsuit?"

"There was a spare in the bay," she said.

"John's gonna be here soon," Isaac said. "We'll have to explain you."

"Ricky," Naomi said. "Before he gets here, I need to tell you something..."

***

John flew the Fire Flyer and his few jets back to the M.A.D. Hangar. He got out and headed towards the M.A.D. Bunker to check on Ricky.

He had to admit, Ricky had proven himself in his eyes. A man who would fight his hardest – even under such injuries – had guts.

He arrived at the M.A.D. Bunker. Isaac was standing near his console. Ricky was seated with Naomi standing next to him.

He was surprised to see what she was wearing.

"Naomi?" John said, puzzled. He turned to Isaac "How can she..."

"I'm Maggie niece," Naomi piped in. "My D.N.A. is a close enough match."

Isaac nodded.

"I see," John said. "Thank you, Naomi. I know this must be difficult."

Naomi stood silent, her eyes locked on his – though they had tears in them.

"I don't expect you to forgive me," John said to her. "Nothing will bring Maggie back..."

John's eyes teared up as he choked on his words. Naomi's expression softened – just a bit.

Isaac patted John's shoulder to attempt to comfort him. John

148

calmed himself a bit.

John watched as Ricky put his arm around Naomi's waist.

Keep her safe, Ricky, John thought to himself.

A silence followed. Isaac piped up.

"The repairs have already begun to the M.A.D. machines," he said. They looked over and saw the mini tanks beginning to reconstruct themselves.

John nodded. "Excellent," he said, focusing himself. "Let's go get something to eat. All of us."

There was a set of nods at his suggestion.

"Naomi, Isaac, the Captain and I will catch up," Ricky said. Naomi nodded to him, and she left with Isaac.

After they left, Ricky stood up with a slight wince. He walked up to John and stared him straight in the eyes.

John steeled himself. "Is there something you wanted to say to me, Ricky?" he asked him.

"There is," Ricky replied. "I have to protect Naomi now. I'm all she has now that Maggie is gone."

Ricky took a deep breath. "So, if you put your hands on Naomi again – you're a dead man," he said simply.

John blinked. *He's not a boy anymore,* he realized.

John gave him a short nod, and they left together for the Great Chamber.

Chapter 32

John and Ricky arrived at the Great Chamber feeling ravenous. After filling their trays, they made their way to where Isaac and Naomi were sitting. John sat down next to Isaac. Ricky sat down next to Naomi. She gave him a look, and he nodded.

"I wish people would stop staring at me," Naomi said as she continued eating.

John stop mid-bite and he looked around.

Sure enough, people sitting nearby looked and whispered to one another. The words 'too young' and 'kid' could be heard.

Ricky looked around and gave a snort.

"Easy," John said to him. He stood up and addressed the hall.

"I'm sure we can all do something other than staring at Ms. Reins." John said sharply.

The people nearby slowly turned their heads and concentrated on their trays.

"Thanks," Naomi said to John as he sat down. He gave her a smile.

"Least I can do," he said. "I'll be speaking with Mr. Juniper in the Agro department. I need you focused on your M.A.D. duties from here on out."

Naomi nodded. John frowned.

"I wish I had time to more formally announce your appointment to the M.A.D., but I do have to get the Captain's funeral set up," he told them all. "I would like to include Maggie in that as well. I will be working on the preparations this afternoon."

They all nodded in agreement.

***

After John and Isaac left to handle their respective duties, Ricky and Naomi went off together. They didn't have a plan to go anywhere in particular – they just wanted to be together.

As they walked down the corridors, people glanced at them both as they walked by. Naomi cringed at the attention. Ricky looked at her in concern.

"Are you gonna be able to handle this?" he asked her.

"I guess I don't have a choice," she replied. "I had to do it to save you and John."

"Hey, and don't think I forgot that," he told her. He leaned in and kissed her on the cheek.

"AH!" he gasped, as he grabbed at his ribs.

"Are you OK?" she asked in concern.

"I'm fine," he said. "Don't worry about it."

They walked for a while more. Then, Ricky spoke up again.

"You know, I think they may have been saying 'too young' and 'kid' about me too," he said to her somberly.

"Well," she said cynically, "It's not like either of us is *old!*"

"I'm serious," he retorted. "I can't believe this has happened to us. You know...everything. The aliens, the attacks, and the M.A.D...."

He held his M.A.D. Black up.

"...and I'm part of it." he said seriously. "I don't think I would have chosen me at all."

Naomi stopped walking. She held Ricky's arm, and he stopped as well.

"Ricky," she said to him. She took a breath. "I wouldn't have chosen this either, but, people are depending on us now – whether they appreciate it or not."

Ricky smiled.

"You know," he told her. "You always say the sweetest things."

"Glad to see you two are alright," a voice said in front of them.

They both turned to see Dr. Duncan striding towards them.

"So, you're in the M.A.D. now too, I see," Dr. Duncan said pointing his finger at Naomi, his words full of malice. "Wonderful! Just wonderful! I'm so glad to know that the fate of humanity rests with you *kids*."

"Hey," Ricky said darkly, *"back off."*

Dr. Duncan focused on Ricky. "How did it feel when Captain Rylund beat the shit out of you?" he said sternly.

Ricky said nothing. Naomi flushed.

"Yeah, I saw that, remember?" Dr. Duncan sneered, crossing his arms. "I don't trust him. Bit of a loose cannon, if you ask me."

Ricky breathed deep. Naomi watched as he walked up to Dr. Duncan.

"I trust him," Ricky said simply.

Naomi walked up next to him. She nodded.

With that, they both left Dr. Duncan standing there. He turned and watched them go.

Well, I don't, he thought to himself. He then strode off down the hall.

        ***

"I would like to setup the funeral this afternoon," John told Mr. Hall in his office. "I want to get the business out of the way as soon as possible."

Joseph nodded to his friend, making some notes on the paper in front of him. His expression seemed tense.

"I should tell you that security has been dealing with some hostilities among the colonists," Joseph said, leaning back in his chair. "We've been able to contain them thus far. It seems that losing Captain Orvis and Dr. Cullen – one of the M.A.D. members – made some folks panic about their safety."

John nodded. Though it had not been formally announced, Maggie, being one of the colony's doctors, would have been noticed missing immediately by her patients – not to mention seeing Naomi in the blue-striped M.A.D. jumpsuit.

"Project M.A.D. is still protecting the colony," John assured him.

"I know and so does my staff," Joseph said. A frown creased

his forehead.

"Joseph," John asked him, "something else is wrong, isn't there?"

Joseph took a deep breath in his chair. He leaned forward.

"John, it is true you nearly beat Ricky Plik to death?" he asked flatly.

John blinked. *How would he think to ask that?* he thought to himself.

Joseph sat silently at his chair, waiting for the answer to his question. Joseph and John had been through a lot together. Lying wasn't something they did.

"Yes," John answered. "I did."

"And why did you do that, *Captain?*" Joseph asked him seriously.

John was taken aback by the change to formality. He told him in the most straightforward manner about his feelings for Maggie, Ricky's lack of discipline during the battle, and, finally, of his own pain and loss at Maggie's death.

When John finished, Joseph sat back in his chair again.

"I have to admit," Joseph said solemnly, "I would have done the same given the circumstances."

John nodded.

"John," Joseph said, going informal again, "before you arrived, Dr. Duncan came and told me what had happened in the M.A.D. Bay."

That son of a bitch, John thought.

"He plans to tell the other department chairs, John," Joseph warned. "He wants to replace you with someone he feels could lead the colony better than you could."

Before John could protest, Joseph spoke again.

"Don't worry," he told him. "I trust you. But, I can't speak for the other department chairs. He would need their majority vote to replace you."

"Who does he want to lead the colony?" John asked, though the answer was on his lips as he asked the question.

"Himself," Joseph said.

Chapter 33

Dr. Isaac Torre stood solemnly at the funeral.

Captain Glenn Orvis and Dr. Maggie Cullen's body lay silently in their coffins. The colonists walked by silently as they paid their respects to them.

Nearby, Ricky Plik stood with his arm around Naomi Reins. She was weeping openly, and Ricky stood strong for her. Captain John Rylund stood with the department chairs around him. Tears were in his eyes as well. But, he managed to maintain his strong composure.

Dr. Torre let his eyes look over the department chairs...

What the... Isaac thought to himself.

His eyes had fallen on Dr. Duncan. Unlike most of the assembled crowd – he seemed *happy*. He stood with nearly half of the department chairs in a group slightly separate from John and the other department chairs.

What's all that about? Isaac wondered.

After roughly an hour or so, the crowds began to disperse and head back to their respective duties or to their quarters. Isaac started to leave when his beeper went off.

He looked at and gasped.

He sprinted off to his laboratory.

It finally broke the code! He thought.

He arrived at his laboratory in a few minutes.

It did! He thought. *It cracked the code!*

***

The next morning, John, Ricky, and Naomi were seated at breakfast in the Great Chamber, the events of yesterday still on their minds.

Suddenly, their M.A.D.s started buzzing. They tensed, as well as the colonists in the tables nearby. However, no alarms were going off.

John picked up his M.A.D. Red and said, "Isaac, what's happening? Are we under attack?"

"No Captain!" Isaac said. His voice was full of panic. "But, I need you all to come to my laboratory right now!"

"Is something wrong, Isaac?" John asked him, hearing the panic in his voice.

"JUST GET DOWN HERE! ALL THREE OF YOU!"

***

After depositing their trays off, John led Ricky and Naomi to Isaac's laboratory.

"What do you think he wants?" Naomi asked.

"Knowing him, he probably wants to show us a new invention," Ricky said. "He loves showing off his new stuff." Then, having a thought, he added. "Maybe he has something to help out M.A.D.!"

"As the attacks have just gotten more intense," John said. "That would be helpful."

They arrived at Isaac's laboratory – John knocked on the door once...

...and Isaac yanked the door open.

"Isaac, you look terrible!" John said to him in concern.

Ricky and Naomi looked at him. He did look terrible. Bags hug under his eyes, and his hair, usually blond and pointy, was shaggy and unkempt. And, he was sporting an uncharacteristic five o'clock shadow.

"Have you been up all night?" John said to him.

Isaac took a moment to nod his head. "Get inside. We have

155

something to talk about."

He ushered them inside, and Isaac had them sit down around a table.

He sat down with them. His seat was surrounded with coffee cups and many printed pages of text. He was breathing heavy, calming himself.

"Is...everything alright, Isaac?" Ricky ventured.

"I have discovered something...," Isaac began. "It concerns M.A.D. and the entire colony's future...hell, the future of humanity!"

John, Ricky, and Naomi tensed.

Isaac put his hands on the table and continued.

"When I created the M.A.D.," he said. "I based the letters, M.A.D., off the symbols I saw on the alien programming code. Since the time I saw that origin code, I have had my computers working to crack the code and translate it so I could understand what the objective of the aliens is. Last night, I finally succeeded..."

He laid his hand on the papers on the table.

"I've been up all night reading it," he added.

"We see that," Naomi said, her eyes looking to the coffee cups.

"Oh yes, I forgot," Isaac said. He grabbed one of the cups and took a sip.

Putting the cup down, he took another deep breath and continued.

"The M.A.D. I discovered in the origin code...stands for the Mechanized Automaton Destroyers."

"The...*what?*" Ricky said, confused.

"The Mechanized Automaton Destroyers," Isaac repeated. "From the best I can make from the translation, there was a race of aliens who depleted the resources of their planet. They decided to create the M.A.D. to capture and harvest the resources from other worlds. This force would be able to rebuilt itself using the resources it had harvested. That is why the M.A.D.'s I created from that technology do the same thing."

"Why create an attacking force?" Naomi asked him.

"They probably didn't want to get their hands dirty," Isaac suggested. "Think about it. Some of the worlds the M.A.D. would attack would have life on them. So, they took the resources they wanted by force."

"But," John interrupted. "Why are the aliens still attacking? They basically have the world conquered at this point. There is really no need to attack our small colony."

"It's part of the M.A.D.'s coding," Isaac said. "To take the resources safely from other worlds, the M.A.D. must destroy the dominant sentient life of the planet. In this case, Homo Sapiens. Since we still exist on this planet, the M.A.D. will continue to attack us until we are gone. That is why they keep attacking the colony. Once we are gone, the aliens can come and gather resources or resettle here."

"Couldn't we talk to the guy in charge of all this?" Ricky offered. "Make some kind of deal?"

Isaac chuckled weakly.

"That's the big thing I wanted to tell you all...," Isaac said, drawing in a breath. "Based on the records I can tell of where the M.A.D. sends their signals back to, which I can only presume to be the home world...it's in a galaxy that collapsed centuries ago..."

John, Ricky, and Naomi looked puzzled.

"Then, shouldn't they stop?" John offered.

"No, their mission isn't complete," Isaac said nervously.

"What mission?" Ricky said.

"To capture and harvest resources from other worlds to support the home world," Isaac said simply.

"But," John said, getting frustrated by the conversation, "their home world doesn't exist anymore..."

"...THEY DON'T KNOW THAT!" Isaac shouted in exasperation.

Ricky and John's faces turned chalk white. Naomi gasped. The realization of Isaac's words dawning on her.

"So," Naomi said slowly. "They want our world...for their race...that doesn't exist anymore?"

Isaac nodded.

Naomi took the words in. John and Ricky sat silently. Naomi had a growing fear in her heart. She decided to voice it.

"These are all just machines attacking us, aren't they?" she asked.

Isaac nodded, biting his lip.

"There are no aliens in them..." Naomi said in shock.

Isaac nodded again, more vigorously this time.

John's face was intense, the weight of the situation on his mind.

"No wonder we haven't seen any aliens in the wreckage of the downed fighters," John said solemnly.

Ricky looked stricken.

"So, they won't stop...until we're all dead?" Ricky said in disbelief.

"...and they have the resources of every world they have conquered since their creation," Isaac finished.

At that moment, the alarms blared. The Mechanized Automaton Destroyers were back.

Chapter 34

"What kind of attack is this time?" John asked Isaac quickly.

Isaac walked over to his computer and brought up some radar screens.

"There are attacking from all fronts this time!" he said in panic. "There are air craft, subs, and a ground force!"

"And us?" Ricky said, picking himself up with John.

Isaac hit a few more buttons.

"Eh...this doesn't look good," Isaac said. "All of our forces are at roughly 50% capacity or less right now. This is gonna be a rough one."

John was already heading towards the door with Ricky following behind him. They were at the door when Ricky stopped and looked at Naomi. Ricky tugged at John's shoulder to halt him.

She was still seated.

I got into the Aqua Marine to help Ricky, she thought. *I didn't have to fight anything off before. I don't know if I can do this.*

Ricky and John had walked back over to her.

"Naomi," John said to her. "It's time to go."

She looked at him, her face pale with fear.

Ricky saw it to, and he got down next to her (his ribs aching). "I know your scared Naomi," he said to her softly. "I know you can do this."

Naomi was silent.

"Be brave like Maggie," he said to her.

She blinked at her aunt's name.

"B-But..." she stammered.

"No 'buts' Naomi," Ricky said to her. "Everyone is counting on us. Captain Rylund, the colonists...and me."

Naomi seemed to steel herself.

"Alright, but I still don't want to die!" she said in panic.

"Hey, I don't either," Ricky said solemnly. "I wanna be with you till..."

He stopped mid-sentence. He made up his mind in an instant.

"Marry me." he asked her simply.

Naomi's eyes lit up. "ARE YOU FUCKING SERIOUS?!" she said incredulously. It was the last thing she expected to hear at that moment – especially from him. Alarms blared around them.

Ricky nodded once, his stomach doing jumps.

John had been watching.

"Naomi," John said firmly, her eyes turning to him. "Say yes and get to the Aqua Marine."

Naomi turned back to Ricky. "YES!" she said to Ricky excitedly, tears in her eyes.

John cleared his throat. *While I have the chance...*

"By the power vested in me as Captain of the Terra colony," John said formally. "I now pronounce you man and wife. Ricky, you may kiss the bride."

Ricky and Naomi kissed.

"That was rather rushed, wasn't it?" Isaac pointed out.

John turned to him and lifted an eyebrow. He pointed to the flashing reds lights around them.

"Oh, right!" Isaac said hurriedly.

***

John headed off to the M.A.D. Hangar along with Isaac, Naomi headed to the M.A.D. Bay., and Ricky headed to the M.A.D. Bunker.

They loaded themselves into their M.A.D.s, and headed out – Isaac was going to watch the three battles from the console in M.A.D. Hangar.

This is gonna be a rough one, he thought to himself.

John had shot out of the hangar with his mini-jets, firing and flying with all the skill he had.

"They are definitely giving it all they have this time!" John said over the M.A.D. "Ricky! Naomi! How are things going down there?"

Down in the Aqua Marine, Naomi had her hands full. The enemy subs fired furious at her. She was firing back, but many of her subs had fallen. None had gotten past her...yet.

"DAMMIT!" she yelled in fury.

Ricky, hearing her scream, switched his view to show her radar.

"Naomi!" Ricky said to her. "Put your mini subs in front of you. Use them as a shield to block the attacks and yourself!"

"Oh, got it!" Naomi responded, and she moved her subs into position.

"Just *concentrate*, Naomi," Ricky told her as calmly as he could, still focusing on his ground battle. "Just concentrate on intercepting the enemy fire."

Naomi focused her efforts on that. She found it easier...though not much. The explosions sounded and flashed all around her.

Ricky was tense in the Dirt Driller. He had made a defensive line in front of colony to block the tanks moving forward, and he was also guarding the ocean side as well. His ribs were still aching in pain.

I'm gonna keep you safe, Naomi, he thought to himself.

The battle raged on. Isaac watched from his console. He watched horrified as enemy fighters took out a jet here, a tank there, a sub there...*holy crap*, he thought. *Hang in there everybody!*

John was probably fairing the worst. He had been hit a few times and the mini jets came up and began their repairs. His remaining forces were dodging with all the skill he could manage.

He checked the radar of the others just to see how they were managing. At that moment, he noticed Ricky's enemy tanks moving into a peculiar formation.

Oh no, he realized to himself.

He examined his radar quickly. He had barely any other jets in the air.

So, he thought, *this is it...*

He took a deep breath.

"Ricky, Naomi," he said over his M.A.D. Red. "You need to keep the people safe for me..."

"What?" Ricky said, confused. Then, on examining the radar, the realization of his words dawned on him.

"JOHN!" he shouted.

"JOHN NO!" Isaac yelled.

"WHAT'S HAPPENING?!" Naomi screamed.

Everyone, John thought just before impact. *I gave it all I had...*

Ricky watched in horror as some of the enemy tanks fired upwards into the air and collided with the Fire Flyer.

"ARGHHHHHH!" John scream sounded over the radio static.

The Fire Flyer, smoking and debris falling from it, plummeted down and crashed hard into the ground in a explosion of fire and dirt.

Isaac had the gun turrets of the colony fire upon the remaining enemy air craft. Without the Fire Flyer in the air, the shots now fired without caution, and the enemy air craft took a severe beating.

Ricky was furiously blowing through the enemy tanks.

I have to get to John! he thought. *He has to be alright!*

Naomi continued her defense in the ocean. She steadily was whittling down the enemy subs.

"RICKY!" she called to him. "IS JOHN ALRIGHT!?"

"I'M GONNA CHECK!" he yelled to her. "JOHN! JOHN!" he called over the M.A.D. Black.

He heard no response.

In the lab, Isaac was tense and filled with dread.

Ricky burst through the enemy tanks, their numbers scattering and fleeing at his onslaught.

He drove the Dirt Driller over to the wreckage of the Fire Flyer. He got himself up and flew out the door of the Dirt Driller, jumping to the ground. His ribs were in agony. He grabbed at them and limped as fast as he could to the wreckage.

"JOHN!" he yelled. "CAN YOU HEAR ME?!"

He plunged himself into the smoke of the wreckage – coughing and gasping for air. He got to the metal interior of the Fire Flyer, and he climbed up onto the wing. He finally found the shattered glass cockpit as the view cleared and looked inside.

John's bloodied body laid there, Maggie's fishing lure necklace stuck out of his pocket. A large rock face had broken through the Fire Flyer floor as he crashed, and it had impacted his body. Shattered glass covered his face and torso. Ricky noticed an arm bone sticking out from the skin and torn through his jumpsuit. His stomach turned.

On the floor of the Fire Flyer, the M.A.D. Red lay shattered.

Chapter 35

Ricky brought John's body into the Dirt Driller – all the while groaning at the pain in his ribs. Climbing back into the driver's seat, he drove it back to the M.A.D. Bunker. What remained of his mini-tanks followed him back in.

Isaac was there waiting for him.

"Where's John?! What happened?!" he asked Ricky frantically.

Ricky had a hold of John's body and was dragging him out the door and onto the platform.

"OH MY GOD!" Isaac moaned.

"HELP ME!" Ricky yelled to him, his face covered in tears.

With Ricky holding John's arms, Isaac came and grabbed his legs. Isaac felt squeamish seeing the blood covering John's body and the broken bone sticking out of his arm.

They brought John's body down to the bunker floor. Ricky and Isaac placed the body on the ground – all their clothes now covered in blood.

Ricky and Isaac looked at the body. They knew that John was beyond hope.

At that moment, Naomi came into the bunker. She was anxious. The battle had been fierce, and she felt shaky and nauseous as she did before.

She saw Ricky and Isaac turn to look at her.

"Hey what...OH GOD, NO!" she screamed as she saw the

body.

Naomi ran over to them and stared at John's broken and bloodied body. Then, she saw the blood covering Ricky's jumpsuit and Isaac's lab coat. She grabbed her stomach...trying to stop the queasiness...

...but she failed and vomited on the floor.

Ricky walked over to Naomi, rubbing her back.

"Isaac, are there some towels or something in here?" Ricky asked him.

Isaac ran over to a closet nearby. He grabbed some towels and ran back over.

He tossed one to Ricky who began to wipe the blood off his jumpsuit, though the staining was still evident. After Ricky had wiped up the blood on him as best he could, he put his arms around Naomi and stood her up.

"You OK?" he asked her as Isaac put a few towels on her vomit.

She nodded. "I...don't believe it...he's dead." she said.

"I know," Ricky said, holding her. Tears were in his eyes.

John's eyes were still open. Ricky bend down and pushed them closed with his fingers.

He stood back up.

They all looked at each other. They were all thinking the same thing. *Now what?*

At that moment, the door to the M.A.D. Bunker opened up, and Joseph Hall strode in purposefully.

"I need to speak with John immediately," he demanded. "I noticed he hadn't returned to the M.A.D. Hangar so I..."

He stopped speaking when he saw all the blood. He walked over and knelt down next to his old friend.

For a few minutes, no one said anything.

Joseph eventually stood up, his eyes watering. He took a deep breath.

"He can't be replaced, can he?" he said simply.

"No," Isaac said. "The D.N.A. lock on the M.A.D. Red can't be overridden..."

"Also....," Ricky said. He pulled the broken M.A.D. Red out of his pocket and handed it to Isaac.

"Dammit," Joseph said. "So, that means we have *two*

situations to deal with..."

"Oh, it gets *better*?" Ricky said bitterly.

Ricky was tense, and Naomi looked puzzled. Isaac, however, had a hunch.

"Dr. Duncan?" Isaac offered.

Mr. Hall nodded. "More accurately, *Captain Duncan*," Mr. Hall said resignedly.

"WHAT?" Naomi said incredulously. "I don't understand..."

Joseph explained quickly the conversation he had had with John earlier that day. Ricky listened intently but said nothing.

"So, that's why those folks stood apart from John at the funeral," Isaac concluded.

Joseph nodded.

"While we were in the security barracks," Joseph explained. "Dr. Duncan managed to convince the department chairs he needed to elect him as the new Captain of the colony."

"Oh that's just great!" Naomi said fiercely. "I am not taking orders from that prick!"

Joseph raised an eyebrow.

"I have no intention of doing so either," he said simply.

Naomi looked at him curiously.

"What?" he told her. "You think I like that asshole?! Trust me, the last thing I wanted was for him to be in charge. Men like that seek authority for the power it gives them. I've seen it before."

"You should all know," he continued. "My men in security department are all dedicated to keeping this colony safe. To that end, Project M.A.D. is still our best chance...despite..."

His voice trailed off as he glanced as John's lifeless body.

"What are we going to do about John's body?" Ricky asked.

"If the colonists find out we have lost our primary air defense," Joseph said sternly. "Full-on panic will ensue. I don't want that to happen."

They were all silent for a moment.

"We can't just leave the body here!" Naomi protested.

Isaac's mind was racing. He had an idea. *This is a long shot,* he thought.

"Mr. Hall," Isaac said. "Escort Dr. Duncan here to the M.A.D. Bunker."

"WHAT?!" they all shouted.

166

Isaac waited a moment for them all to recover from their outburst.

"I have an idea," he told them. "Listen..."

He told them his idea quickly. One by one, they nodded their heads.

"Alright then," Isaac said. "Ricky, Naomi, why don't you to head to lunch. You must be starving. Also, Ricky, you should grab an extra jumpsuit and change before you go."

Ricky looked down at his bloodied jumpsuit.

"There is an extra one in the closet there," Isaac said, pointing with his finger.

Ricky changed himself quickly. Joseph headed off to fetch Dr. Duncan.

Ricky took Naomi's arm. After one last look at John, they both left the M.A.D. Hangar.

***

Ricky and Naomi arrived at the Great Chamber for lunch, neither of them saying much to each other. They gathered their trays and sat down.

"Naomi!" a voice called. "How did the fight go?"

Naomi jumped and turned in her seat. Mr. Juniper was walking towards them.

"I didn't mean to frighten you!" he said apologetically. "I just wanted to make sure you're alright! You are, aren't you?"

"Um...sure!" she said with nervous enthusiasm.

Mr. Juniper eyed them both strangely.

"Where is John, by the way?" he asked casually.

Naomi hesitated.

"Oh, I see," Mr. Juniper said. "He must be all *banged up* what with Duncan taking on being the Captain now."

And with that, Mr. Juniper walked off to join some of the others from the Agro sector.

Naomi looked back at Ricky. He was breathing heavy.

"Are you alright, Ricky?" she asked him.

"I'll be OK," he replied. "I just wish he didn't say *banged up*."

Naomi nodded and went back to eating.

"Are you alright, Mrs. Plik?" he asked her, giving her a grin.

"Yeah...OH!" she yelped. She had forgotten with the M.A.D. battle and the loss of John that she was now married to Ricky. She gave him a glowing smile. He would always know how to make her smile.

They both laughed. It felt good to laugh.

"I'm still not feeling my best," Naomi told Ricky as they were finishing up. "I want to visit the infirmary and have them check me out..."

"...do you want me to go with you?" Ricky asked her in concern.

"No, I'd like to go alone," she told him. "I have some thinking to do."

Ricky nodded, they kissed, and Naomi walked off towards the infirmary.

***

Dr. Duncan glared at Isaac and Joseph.

"So, let me see if I understand this," Dr. Duncan said crossing his arms. "John Rylund, the former Captain of the Terra colony, is dead. He was the pilot of the Fire Flyer – our air defense force. You want me to remove the body, take it to the infirmary and treat it for burial...*and tell no one that he's died?*"

"Yes," Isaac said firmly.

Dr. Duncan started chuckling, and he walked about non-nonchalantly.

"I am the Captain of the colony now," he said simply. "I will certainly have the body treated at the infirmary. But...to keep it quiet..."

He whipped his head quickly to face them.

"ARE YOU BOTH MAD!?" Dr. Duncan roared. "We've lost the primary air defense! You cannot possibly expect me to keep this quiet!"

Dr. Duncan was pacing furiously back and forth.

"I won't do it!" he told them fiercely. "You have no authority to make me do so. Mr. Hall, I order you..."

"...I'm afraid I can't let you tell the colony of John's death," Joseph interrupted fiercely.

Dr. Duncan looked at him with fury.

"YOU OBEY MY ORDERS NOW!" he yelled. "UNLESS YOU'VE FORGOTTEN!"

"No," Joseph said. "Hear me, *Captain* Duncan. My duty is maintain the peace and security within the Terra colony. The people must feel they are safe. If they learn that the air defense is gone, they will panic. They will riot. What will you tell them then?"

Dr. Duncan said nothing.

"My security team and I will keep the peace within Terra, and you must as well," Joseph said.

"But...," Dr. Duncan began to protest.

"NO BUTS!" Joseph said sharply. "Also, so you know, none of my security personnel feel loyalty to you. Our duty is to Terra alone."

Dr. Duncan's face paled. He was silent for several seconds.

Then, he began to breathe deeply. "Very well. I will keep it quiet myself, but I cannot promise about my assistants. The medics who saw to Maggie and Ricky had a hard time keeping that whole mess quiet."

"I'll stay here while you tend to the body," Joseph said. "Bring your medics to assist you, and we, *together*, will explain the situation to them."

Dr. Duncan nodded and left – giving Joseph and Isaac a dark glare.

Chapter 36

Ricky was walking down the corridors of the colony in deep thought, when suddenly...

"RICKY!"

Ricky looked around and saw a young boy running towards him.

"MARK!" a voice called after him from down the hall.

The boy ran up and wrapped his arms around his legs.

"HEY!" Ricky said in surprise.

Hearing footsteps, Ricky looked up and saw a woman striding towards them.

"MOM! IT'S HIM! IT'S RICKY PLIK!" Mark yelled excitedly to his mother.

"*Let him go, Mark!*" the woman scolded. She grabbed the boy off Ricky and said: "I'm terribly sorry! Mark was just so excited to finally meet you! He's been very ill the last few days, and he never got the chance to see you up close in the Great Chamber during meal times."

Ricky looked down at the boy. He was looking up at him with admiration in his eyes.

A few days ago, I would have loved this kind of attention. But now...

Ricky got down on one knee so he was eye level with the boy. He grunted as his ribs ached again, but he kept a smile on.

"I'm Mark!" he said. "You fight the aliens along with John,

right?"

Yeah, with John, Ricky thought sadly.

"Yeah, I fight the aliens," Ricky said to him soberly. "Pretty dangerous stuff."

"What do you fight with?" Mark asked excitedly. "Do you fight with jets just like John?"

"No, I fight with tanks," he told him. "I take care of things on the ground."

"Tanks! That's awesome!" he said. "I bet no one can beat you..."

"That's quite enough, Mark," his mother said. "I'm sure that Ricky probably wants to spend some time resting what with the battle this morning."

"Aw...," Mark moaned.

The woman started to walk Mark away. Mark waved excitedly back to Ricky, and Ricky waved back at him with a smile.

After they were out of sight, Ricky continued on walking. He eventually arrived at his quarters and let himself in. He sat himself down in one of his chairs and turned on a music CD. Calm music filled the air.

That kid really looks up to me, he thought to himself.

Everyone does...

They look up to us...to me...

Ricky reached over and turned the music off. A moment later, he grabbed his radio and threw it against the wall, shattering it to pieces.

His ribs flared in agony. He ignored it. Adrenaline fueled him.

Ricky grabbed the other chair and flung in against the wall – smashing it to bits. He did the same to the one he was sitting in. He ran over to his bed and flipped it. The sheets flew off and the frame landed upside down.

He was breathing heavy and tears filled his eyes.

He reached out and felt his hand grab something and, swinging it like a club, he brought it down hard on the floor...

... and he heard the strings twang and the wood of the guitar splinter and smash.

Ricky stopped, still holding the guitar handle. Tears flowed down his face.

He sat down himself down on the floor and cried. He didn't know how long he sat there, pondering over everything...

Maggie's dead. John's dead...we have no air defense...

Only Naomi and I are left to defend the colony...

AH!

And my ribs...

I want to find some peace, he thought. *And I only know one place where I can find it now...*

He got up and left his ruined apartment.

The only place where my actions mean something...

***

Naomi was in one of the patient rooms of the infirmary sitting on the bed. She was waiting to be seen by the next available doctor.

Whoever it is, she thought sadly. *It won't be Maggie.*

Soon, there was a knock on the door.

"Come in," she said.

And in walked Dr. Duncan with a clipboard in his hand.

"YOU!?" she said incredulously.

"Yes," Dr. Duncan said with a sneer. "I thought – since you needed some medical care – this would be a golden opportunity to have a little chat."

He shut the door firmly.

"What do you want with me, *Herman*?" she told him fiercely.

"That's *Captain Duncan* to you!" he snapped at her. "Or did you not get the memo?"

Naomi fumed. "You think I want to discuss my problems with you?!"

They both glared at each other.

After a few moments, Dr. Duncan took a deep breath sat himself down in the chair.

"I want to help you, Naomi," he said evenly. "Please?"

"FUCK OFF!" she roared at him.

Dr. Duncan flung his clipboard against the wall with a bang. He'd put up with a lot in the past few week, but this was the final straw.

He stood up. "I have watched as the events have unfolded in

this colony," Dr. Duncan said fiercely. "And I, along with the colony, have been powerless to influence any of it. John Rylund was selected to join Project M.A.D., soon followed by your aunt..."

Dr. Duncan's eyes watered with tears.

"Then," he continued, his voice dripping with sarcasm. "Who shows up to join the ranks? Why, a young party boy! It was wonderful! Then, guess what happened? OUR CAPTAIN DIED! And who replaces him? Why, John Rylund, of course! Because that was *clearly* the only choice!"

Naomi sat listening to his tirade in silence.

"And what a choice it was!" he continued. "His first order of business? Why, get Maggie killed *and* beat the shit out of your little boy toy! And despite that, you join up with M.A.D. as well!"

Dr. Duncan stopped, breathing heavy. His face flushed.

"John Rylund is dead," he said simply. "I am now the Captain of this colony, and dammit, despite everything, I *will* be shown some respect. So, you had better get used to that – YOU IMPERTINENT LITTLE GIRL!"

Dr. Duncan stopped his tirade and focused on Naomi's face...

...she was crying. She had covered her face with her hands.

That felt so good to get that all out, he thought. *But, I would never have made Maggie cry like this.*

Naomi continued crying for several minutes. Dr. Duncan said nothing.

Finally, Naomi wiped her face and said: "Do you feel better n-now, you f-fucker?"

Dr. Duncan bowed his head slightly, saying nothing.

"Ricky and I are risking our lives to defend this colony," she said, her voice cracking. "Do you even care? Does t-that mean nothing to you?"

Dr. Duncan looked up into her eyes.

"Yes," he said meekly. "Yes it does."

He stood up straighter.

"Naomi," he said firmly. "As Captain of this colony, I must have you in good health. Will you permit me to help you?"

As much as she hated him still, she sensed he was genuine. She nodded.

"Then tell me why you're here." he said.

She told him how she had been feeling after the last two

M.A.D. combats, with the queasiness, the nausea, and the vomiting she had just had earlier that day.

Dr. Duncan listened intently, and, after having retrieved his clipboard and taking a few notes said: "I have an idea as to why you've been feeling the way you have. But, I'd need to run a test or two to be sure..."

***

After she left the infirmary, she headed to the Great Chamber anxious to find Ricky. It was dinnertime, and she searched around the tables but couldn't find him.

After waiting for a few minutes for him to arrive, she gathered up food for herself and Ricky and went off to his quarters.

"Ricky!" she called, rapping on his door.

She heard no response.

She tried turning the knob and found it unlocked. She pushed the door open, and she gasped at the wreckage of the room.

What the hell happened? She wondered. She walked inside and examined the overturned chairs, the flipped bed, the shatter radio, and the broken guitar. *Was he attacked by someone?*

Naomi pulled out her M.A.D. Blue.

"ISAAC!" she called.

"Naomi!" she heard Isaac reply. "What's up?"

"HAVE YOU SEEN RICKY!" she asked in panic. "HIS PLACE HAS BEEN TRASHED!"

"No, I haven't!" he said in concern, hearing her panic. "When did you last..."

"Naomi, it's alright!" she heard Ricky say over the M.A.D. Blue.

"RICKY!" she said. "THANK GOD!! I'm at your quarters, what happened..."

"Come to the M.A.D. Bunker," he said calmly. "Just...come."

Chapter 37

Naomi walked as fast as she could down the corridors to the M.A.D. Bunker.

She opened up the door to the bunker. Looking around, she saw Ricky sitting on top of the Dirt Driller quietly.

Carrying the food with her, she walked up the platform.

"Hey, what's going on?" she asked. "Your room is completely trashed! I mean...more than usual."

Ricky didn't move or speak.

"I didn't see you for dinner, so I brought you some food," she said, holding out the bag for him to see.

He still didn't reply.

"DAMN IT! ANSWER ME!" she yelled.

"Naomi," he said, not moving from his position. "I'd like to take the Dirt Driller outside for a while – just to get away for a bit. Would you come with me?"

The request took her by surprise. "Sure, Ricky," she replied.

They climbed inside the tank (Ricky grunting at his ribs), and he rolled it out of the bunker and away from the colony. Naomi sat herself as comfortably as she could in the cramped space.

Ricky rolled the Dirt Driller past the wreckage of alien craft here and there. They both saw the wreckage of the Fire Flyer. Ricky said nothing as they passed by it.

"That food smells good," he eventually said. "We'll stop here."

Ricky had driven out to the open plains a few miles from the colony. They got out, and they saw that the colony was just visible in the distance.

The sky was clear without any clouds that evening. The stars were all shining, and the bright moon glowed.

The air was warm enough, and Ricky and Naomi climbed back on top of the tank.

"Thanks for bringing the food," Ricky said to her as he unwrapped the packages. "I'm starving."

She smiled at him.

They ate in silence, both of them having a lot on their minds.

After they had finished, Ricky laid back on the tank and looked up at the stars. Naomi followed his lead, and she laid down next to him.

"Now, what happened in your room?" she finally asked him.

Ricky didn't respond.

She nudged him. "Hey," she asked. "What..."

"Because it was meaningless," he said simply.

"What?" Naomi said, puzzled.

"Everything I was...means nothing," he said. "What are we gonna do? John's gone. It's all up to us now."

Naomi saw his eyes fill with tears. He started crying.

She picked herself up and looked at him.

"Ricky...," she said, trying to console him.

He picked himself up, ignoring his ribs.

"EVERYONE'S COUNTING ON US, NAOMI!" he yelled, tears streaming down his face. "The attacks just keep getting worse! You heard Isaac! They're not gonna stop till we're all DEAD! And, with John gone, we don't have air defense anymore!"

He put his head into his hands and wept.

She grabbed a hold of his shoulder.

"Everyone's gonna die...," he said sadly through his tears.

"No they won't!" she said firmly.

Ricky batted her arm away and faced her.

"HOW DO YOU KNOW THAT?!" he shouted at her. "Maggie died! John died! Hell, most of the world has been killed off! What makes us immune!?"

Normally, Naomi would have punched him for shouting at her. But, she had no answer for him.

176

"We have to try," she answered meekly. "For everyone's sake..."

"You know what happened today?" he said to her crassly. "A little kid stopped me in a corridor. He looks up to me. Thinks I'm invincible. That we're gonna save them all..."

Ricky cried more. He couldn't help it.

"I just...can't do this..." Ricky choked, and he pounded his fist on the metal beneath them. "This tank is all I have, Naomi! And...I don't know if I can protect everyone...including you..."

He brought his hand up to her chin. Her eyes were watering up. He kissed her, as tears still flowed down his face.

"You know I would do anything for you," he said, his eyes red from tears. "But, how can I keep you safe from all this? Hell, how can I keep everyone safe!?"

"Hey," she said, her eyes watering. "I don't know if I can keep myself safe. It's terrifying for me, too! But...I have to try...for Maggie and John's sake...for everyone's sake..."

She took a few deep breaths, steeling herself.

"I'm *pregnant*," she told him.

Ricky froze. He leveled his gaze on her.

"*What?*" he said simply, his face paled.

"When I was at the infirmary," she told him, her voice shaky but firm, "They checked my vitals to see why I had been feeling so nauseous and queasy recently. They did some tests, and they found out that I'm pregnant."

Ricky said nothing.

She took a breath and said: "They say it's a girl..."

"...Maggie," Ricky said firmly, his eyes locked with hers. "Her name is Maggie."

Naomi blinked. She didn't question his name choice.

Then, Naomi began to cry.

"MY GOD, RICKY!" she wailed, starting to weep. "I...I...what if..."

Ricky brought her sobbing face into his chest – trying to calm her. His ribs ached terribly, but he wouldn't let her go. Not now.

He lifted face up. "PLEASE!" he yelled out into the night sky as tears flowed again. "PLEASE! LET US MAKE IT THROUGH THIS! PLEASE!"

Chapter 38

Ricky and Naomi didn't know when they returned to the colony. All they knew is that they were together.

When Ricky returned the Dirt Driller into the bunker, he looked upon what was left of his tank force.

Damn, he thought.

They walked along the empty hallways, and, by unspoken agreement, they spent the night in Naomi's quarters. When they awoke, it was well past breakfast time in the Great Chamber. Starving, they made their way for lunch.

***

Isaac got himself up from bed that morning feeling tired and weary – his mind filled with dread all evening. His clock showed it was well past breakfast.

He took a shower and got his hair the way he liked it. Then, checking himself in the mirror, he headed off to breakfast – hoping some food would cheer him up.

***

Dr. Duncan completed his morning rounds with the department chairs – including Mr. Hall who he desperately wanted to slug in the face.

He sat down at breakfast sulking. He stared out at all the colonists – none of which seemed to pay him any attention. The same thing happened at lunch.

I am the Captain of the Terra colony, he thought to himself. *I will not be ignored...*

***

Isaac arrived at the Great Chamber for lunchtime. He saw Ricky and Naomi sitting at one of the tables.

He gathered his tray and headed to their table.

"Hey," he asked them as he approached. "Good to see you two."

He sat down at the table with them. He noticed that neither of them were talking.

"What happened last night?" he asked them curiously. "I saw the Dirt Driller power up on my system and leave the colony. I knew it had to be you, Ricky, so I didn't raise any alarms. What happened?"

"I NEEDED SOME TIME AWAY FROM EVERYTHING, OK!" Ricky said tersely.

Isaac jumped. "Gee, sorry!"

"It's alright Isaac," Naomi said to him, placing a hand on Ricky's shoulder. "We just needed some time away – the two of us."

Ricky took a breath "We got in late...," he said softly.

"The two of you?" Isaac said in surprise.

Neither Ricky nor Naomi said anything. Isaac nodded.

"I guess things have been a bit crazy lately," Isaac said, digging into his lunch.

"How are you feeling this morning, Isaac?" Naomi asked him, trying to steer the conversation in a different direction.

Isaac struggled for words. He had remembered his encounter with Dr. Duncan, but he didn't feel like mentioning it. He ate in silence for a few minutes before answering.

"I couldn't sleep," he said, bringing his voice down so only they could hear. "What with everything that's been happening, I couldn't relax at all. I checked on the M.A.D. repairs...they are going as fast as they can..."

Both Ricky and Naomi nodded.

"I don't know how long we can keep this up," Isaac sighed.

At that moment, the M.A.D.s went off and alarms blared.

"I guess we're about to find out...," Isaac sighed.

***

They stood up and headed from the Great Chamber together. Isaac checked his personal communicator.

He stopped dead in the corridor. "Whoa....," he said, staring at the screen.

"What is it?" Ricky asked him.

He took off running. Ricky and Naomi stole a glance at one another and ran off after him.

"Isaac! Wait!" they shouted after him.

***

Dr. Duncan had seen the three of them rush off down the corridor after the alarms went off. He strode after them.

Not without me...

***

Ricky and Naomi followed Isaac down the corridors eventually leading to his laboratory.

He got the door opened and switched on his lights. He headed over to his main console and brought up some live feeds of the outside of the colony.

"Oh man," he said.

Ricky and Naomi walked in and stood behind him.

"Isaac, what is it?" Naomi said impatiently.

Isaac pushed his chair away from the screen.

"LOOK!" he yelled, pointing.

Ricky and Naomi stepped forward to get a better view of the video feed that he brought up.

"What the....," Ricky said quietly.

"Holy...shit....," Naomi said, stunned.

Descending from the clouds near the colony was a massive, column shaped machine – many times wider and taller than any

180

skyscraper on Earth. Many aircraft flew around it. The machine pulsed with energy, as the air around it seemed to shimmer and blur like the air on a hot summer day. Smoke and steam billowed out of air vents all around it – like breath.

The giant pillar slid down and crashed into the ground – the entire colony shook at the impact. Looking up, the pillar machine was still stretched up beyond the clouds themselves.

Then, a loud sound vibrated from the machine, and electrical sparks flared from the base on the ground. They all watched on the monitor as the ground around the machine began to turn brown and then gray. The plant life shriveled and died as the circle of energy around the machine grew wider.

"WHAT IS IT DOING?!" Naomi yelled in panic.

Isaac checked his computer monitors.

"It's...I don't believe this...," Isaac said in disbelief. "It's...absorbing life energy from the planet itself!"

"*Well, that's just wonderful!*" a voice called out from behind them.

They all jumped and turned. Dr. Duncan stood in the doorway behind them. He entered and slammed the door shut.

He walked forward casually. He clapped his hands together and rubbed them vigorously. "So," he said in mock enthusiasm. "What's the plan people?"

Ricky's eyebrow's tensed, and Naomi scowled.

Isaac was the first to speak. "Dr. Duncan..."

"CAPTAIN DUNCAN!" Dr. Duncan roared at them. "AND DON'T YOU FORGET IT!"

"*Captain Duncan*," Isaac corrected darkly. "As you can see, we have a situation..."

"NO SHIT!" Dr. Duncan said, striding forward. "Another fine mess, I see!"

Ricky and Naomi stared him down.

"Oh!" he said, seeing them eying him. "It's the young people who will save the world!"

Dr. Duncan stepped up to the monitor.

"So, tell me, youngsters," he said, pointing to the monitor. "How do you plan on stopping *that?!*"

Ricky and Naomi said nothing.

"Figures," he said angrily. "I didn't really expect much at this point. Not with a party boy and his little slut to defend..."

POW!

Ricky slammed his fist into Dr. Duncan's face as hard as he could. Dr. Duncan fell to the floor.

His body lay still.

Isaac stepped over and checked his neck for a pulse.

"You knocked him out cold," Isaac said seriously. Then, he turned and smiled. "Nice one."

"*Asshole*," Ricky said to Dr. Duncan's prone form.

Naomi grasped his hand. He turned to look at her. She was smiling at him.

Isaac stood back up and checked his computer again.

"You two had better get going," he told them. "There is an all-out attacking approaching the colony, complete with air, aquatic, and ground forces. I'll get the gun turrets firing with all we have."

He looked back at Dr. Duncan's body. "And I'll take care of him," he added.

Chapter 39

Ricky and Naomi hurried off from the laboratory.

"How will we defend the colony without John?" Naomi said as they marched down the corridor.

Ricky thought about that. His face tense.

"We won't be able to," he said gravely. "Not completely, anyway. I have to deal with the ground forces and you've got the subs to deal with. Then...there's that huge thing."

Naomi shuddered.

"What will we do?" she asked nervously.

"I'm gonna use my tanks to dig a full moat around the colony," he said. "That way, just like you did before, you'll be able to fire out of the water with your torpedoes at the attacking force – but, from any direction. It's not perfect, but its better than nothing."

They stopped in the corridor as they were about to separate.

Ricky looked at her. Her eyes were tearing up.

He held her in his arms.

"We will make it through this," he said to her. He leaned in and kissed her on the lips.

Then, they broke off and ran to their respective M.A.D. machines.

***

Mr. Hall had arrived with security to Isaac's lab. Dr. Duncan was starting to regain consciousness.

Isaac quickly explained what had happened only moments ago. Mr. Hall nodded to his officers.

Dr. Duncan felt arms grasping him and lifting him up. When he finally was on his feet, Mr. Hall stood before him.

"Dr. Duncan," Mr. Hall said to him. "You are being placed into confinement. I will not have anyone harassing the M.A.D. members."

"Let go of me!" Dr. Duncan snapped, struggling in their grip. "I am the Captain of this colony! Let me go!"

"As of this moment, under my authority as head of security, your title is hereby revoked," Mr. Hall said firmly.

Dr. Duncan's eyes grew wide.

"YOU CAN'T DO THIS TO ME! LET ME GO!" he screamed.

No one listened to his pleas. The alarms still blaring around him, he began to shout out hysterics.

"WE HAVE NO AIR DEFENSE!" Dr. Duncan roared. "RYLUND IS DEAD! DON'T YOU ALL SEE? WE'RE ALL GONNA DIE!"

Still screaming, Dr. Duncan was dragged out of the lab.

Mr. Hall turned his attention to Isaac.

"What's the plan, Dr. Torre?" Mr. Hall asked him.

"Keep the colonists in the security barracks for their protection," Isaac said sternly. He pointed to his monitor. "I don't know how this will turn out this time..."

"MY GOD...," Mr. Hall said nervously. "And, what will you do?"

Isaac walked to the door. He turned and gave him a determined look.

"I'm gonna go help save the world," he said. With that, he turned and left.

***

Naomi arrived at the M.A.D. Bay. She climbed into the Aqua Marine and sat down.

Around her neck, she felt for her father's locket.

She breathed deeply for a few moments, steeling herself. She was feeling nauseous again.

"Don't worry, Maggie," she said. "We'll be OK."

She pushed the M.A.D. Blue into the slot and powered up the mini subs.

"Let's do this," She said aloud.

***

Ricky got the M.A.D. Bunker. He stopped and stared at the Dirt Driller.

"It's just you and me, tank." he said. He glanced at his remaining mini tanks – wishing he had more.

"Let's kick some ass," he said with more confidence then he felt.

He climbed inside and set the M.A.D. Black in place. The Dirt Driller hummed to life around him...

...and his ribs ached once more.

***

Isaac arrived at the very highest level of the Terra colony. He approached a door at the end of a hallway. On the pin pad next to the door, he entered a code sequence and pressed his hand to a panel.

An audible ding was heard.

The door slid open, and Isaac walked into a circular room.

He sat himself down on the chair in the middle, and he swung it around and grabbed a control panel. He checked that it could slide left and right swiftly.

"Excellent," he said.

Isaac had designed this room and its weapon system during the early development of the M.A.D. technology. When he went to integrate a D.N.A. Locking system into the controls, the D.N.A. lock chose the first person who touched it...

...and here he was.

With the M.A.D.s he designed afterward, he made himself excluded from that D.N.A. selection.

With all the work he had been doing for the colony, perfecting and completing the M.A.D.s, he had yet to get back and put the finishing touches to this project.

As it stood now, the power source for this weapon was the colony's power itself – having not fully integrated the M.A.D. technology into it. As it was untested, he would never have considered using it unless the colony was in great peril.

"Good a time as any," he said. He flicked some switches, and the machine powered up.

***

Ricky rolled the Dirt Driller and his mini tanks out of the M.A.D. Bunker.

Alright guys, he thought, *just like I said before. Let's kick some ass.*

He watched on his radar as the mini tanks started to drill into the ground. After making a trench deep enough for Naomi's subs, he finally had them breach the ocean side and water flowed in to create a deep moat around the colony.

"That should do it," Ricky said. "How's it look from your end, Naomi?"

Naomi was in the Aqua Marine. She had been watching the mini tanks breach the ocean side where she could see. She now guided some of her mini subs into the moat created.

"It's just fine." she told him. "I'll be able to get them to fire off without a problem!"

"Good," Ricky replied hurriedly. "Because here they come! Get ready!"

On Ricky's radar, the ground and air force approached the colony. His mini tanks had resurfaced from the moat, and he commenced firing upon the enemy – trying to keep them from getting any closer then he felt comfortable with.

Naomi's Aqua Marine was still in the ocean. The enemy subs approached her, and she fired off torpedoes to counter the assault she faced. In addition, she had some of her mini subs in the moat to provide some support fire for Ricky's ground assault.

Ricky was able to hold off the ground forces well enough with Naomi's help...and then the air attacks started in.

The Dirt Driller rocked and shook violently with the air assault – Ricky winced and grabbed his ribs. Tanks exploded around him.

"GOD DAMN IT!" he yelled, as he angled some of his attacks skyward trying to get them off him. However, taking his focus off the ground force let more of the attacks on the ground get through.

Naomi noticed this and started to angle her attacks to compensate.

"OH!" she yelled, as a torpedo in the water crashed into a mini sub near her.

"NAOMI! YOU ALRIGHT?!" Ricky yelled.

"I'M FINE!" she yelled. "BUT WE REALLY ARE OUTMATCHED HERE!"

As Ricky was looking up in the air shooting at the air assault, he suddenly saw a huge blast of lightning shoot across the sky and slam into a pair of fighters. They exploded and fell from the sky.

"WHAT THE...," Ricky said.

"I just saw it on my radar!" Naomi said. "What was that..."

HANG IN THERE YOU TWO!" they heard a familiar voice yell over the radio.

"ISAAC?!" Ricky and Naomi said in surprise.

"I'll handle some of this air assault!" he said. Ricky watched as another lightning blast soared across the sky, knocking out a few more jets from the air.

"What is that thing your firing?" Ricky said, moving his tank windshield so he could look back at the colony.

The top of the colony had lifted up, to reveal a giant ray gun in a metal column.

"I call it the *Torre Turret!*" he told them. "You didn't think I'd let you guys have all the fun, did you?"

Ricky smiled. "Thanks for the help!" he yelled.

"NAOMI!" Isaac said to him. "This cannon thing up here takes power from the colony directly. Guard the hydro-electric plant well, alright?"

"Will do...AHH!" Naomi yelled, as another torpedo came too close for her comfort. "DAMN IT!"

"Hold it together down there!" Ricky told her. "Isaac, what's happening in the colony?"

"Captain Duncan is in confinement. I told Mr. Hall to keep everyone down in the security barracks for protection!" Isaac said evenly, shooting off another blast. "It's the safest place for them right now."

"Yeah, but what about us?!" Ricky said warningly, as he dodged another wave of shots.

Chapter 40

As the battle raged on, Ricky stole glances at the colony.

The outside of the colony was sustaining heavy damage. Shards of the metal coating showed through as the rock of the mountainside was blasted apart.

Hang in there, everybody, he thought to himself.

He looked towards the pillar machine. It continued sucking up of energy from the ground. He could see the brown and dead ground spreading around it. Withered trees dotted the area.

How the hell do you stop something like that? he wondered.

An explosion rocked him from the thought. He realized that, in his observations, he had allowed the enemy tanks to get closer. He blasted many of them and retreated his forces towards the colony to protect it.

I gotta focus, he thought. "Naomi!" he said aloud. "How are things in the water?"

Between focusing on the normal ocean battle near the hydro-electric plant and trying to help defend via the moat, Naomi's concentration was strained.

"I'm doing what I can do here....AHH!" she screamed as another blast erupted one of her subs.

"SHIT! I'm losing it here!"

"FOCUS!" Ricky told her, trying to keep his calm. *How long can we hold this out?*

"ISAAC!" Ricky said. "How's that weapon of yours

working?" He had seen jets falling from the sky, but he hadn't seen any in the last few minutes.

"Just charging it up again!" Isaac said. "I got the normal turrets firing at everything!"

"CHARGING?!" Ricky said in disbelief. "Why do you have to charge it?"

"It takes power straight from the colony," he said. "It doesn't generate its own power like the M.A.D.s do."

"You sound surprisingly calm...," Ricky said nervously as more explosions happened around him.

"ARE YOU KIDDING?!" Isaac said with enthusiasm. "I'M FUCKING TERRIFIED! BUT THIS IS AMAZING!"

"Just keep it together for all our sakes..."

BOOM!

A loud blasting sound roared over the static.

"WHAT WAS THAT?!" Isaac yelled. Ricky heard levers and buttons being frantically pushed. "I've lost all the power to the Torre Turret!"

"A TORPEDO GOT PAST ME!" Naomi yelled in panic. "IT CRASHED INTO THE HYDRO-ELECTRIC PLANT!"

Naomi looked back towards the M.A.D. Bay and saw the sparks and metal raining from the destroyed hydro-electric plant.

"I can't make it fire!" Isaac said in panic. "I don't even have the..."

"ISAAC!" Ricky yelled, as he saw an enemy missile launch towards the top of the colony.

"AHHHHHHHHHHHHHHH!" they heard Isaac yell over static. The top of the tower had exploded in a fiery blast. Metal and rock fell from the structure.

"Isaac! ISAAC!" Ricky yelled.

"WHAT HAPPENED?!" Naomi shouted, as she countered another torpedo fired at her.

"Isaac took a direct hit at the top of the colony!" Ricky said, his nerves on edge. "I lost contact with him!"

***

Up in the ruins of the Torre Turret, Isaac's body lay against the console. Smoke and electric sparks filled the room. A metal bar had fallen onto his back – pinning him down. His forehead had a huge cut in it. His hair was covered in metal scraps and dust.

He wasn't breathing.

***

"Guess it's just us now...AH!" Ricky said, as he dodged another shot and his ribs throbbed. The Dirt Driller was rocking violently.

Naomi's enemy fired upon her more quickly. She was barely able to keep up. In her mind, she had all but abandoned the coverage of the colony.

Ricky saw on his screen the subs surrounding Naomi.

"Get your subs back to you!" he yelled to her. "I'll defend out here!"

"OK!" she said, calling her subs back from the moat.

Ricky was up against the colony now. None of the turrets of the colony were firing with the power gone, and the metal and rock wall was blasted with repeated attacks from the enemy tanks and jets.

Down in the Aqua Marine, Naomi's nerves were getting the best of her. The attacks on her subs keep happening. She kept firing back. The explosions rocked the water around her.

In her repeated counter-attacks of the torpedoes, she missed one aimed straight at her.

"OH MY GOD! RICKY!" Naomi screamed.

"NAOMI!" Ricky yelled, seeing the view on his screen.

He heard the explosion over the static. The Aqua Marine vanished off the radar.

"Naomi! NAOMI!" he yelled in panic.

He heard nothing.

"NAOMIIIIIIIIIIIIIIIIIIIIIIIIIIIIIIIIIIIIIIIII!" he wailed.

Tears filled his eyes. He cried.

She's gone. Naomi's gone...

My daughter's gone...

"Damn you aliens! DAMN YOU!" he yelled.

He looked out and saw the pillar machine in the distance.

Enough of this shit!

He rolled the Dirt Driller as fast as he could towards the

pillar machine. He had the remaining mini tanks provide guard fire on his sides.

Nothing is stopping me from getting into that thing and blowing it to hell!

The mini tanks fell around him.

"COME ON! COME ON!" he yelled furiously. "GET THERE FASTER!"

The Dirt Driller rolled across the brown and black land – and he rolled into the electrical field surrounding the machine.

The Dirt Driller flashed inside with the jolt of electricity. Ricky heard flashes and bangs around him but forced the tank forward.

"COME ON!" he yelled.

He finally got his drill to bore into the pillar machine, digging a hole through the metal shell with sparks flying wildly.

A dark space awaited him inside as he rolled in. The Dirt Driller's interior was smoking badly, and sparks were shooting off everywhere.

With a lurch, the Dirt Driller rolled to a stop. No matter how hard he thought it, he could not make the tank move.

"DAMN IT!" he yelled, taking the helmet off. "Well, let's take a look at this thing."

Ricky grabbed the M.A.D. Black from the console and stepped out to see what the inside of the column looked like.

He stepped out into the tall and mostly hollow space. The machinery inside towered above him. Wires, knobs, buzzers, and switches lit up here and there along the tall walls of the structure.

Just as Isaac said...not a single alien in sight.

Ricky moaned. He didn't realize how badly he was hurting physically. The rocking and explosions of the Dirt Driller combat had irritated his still healing ribs, and he had many burns on his hands and through his jumpsuit from the electric shock field he passed through.

He just stood there and panted.

Suddenly, wires and cables came at him from the shadows. They wrapped around his body. He felt an electric shock go through him. He watched as a wire cable wrapped around his right arm, whipping around till it reached the M.A.D. Black and connected with a jolt...

...and Ricky lost consciousness.

***

On the ocean front surrounding the colony, Naomi's body was washed ashore. The machines attacking the colony took no notice. Blasts of explosions happened all around.

Her blonde hair covered her face. Her gray jumpsuit was damp and had deep blood stains.

Around her neck, the small golden chain held a broken locket fragment. The picture that used to be there was lost in the ocean.

Grasped in her hand, the M.A.D. Blue was shattered and broken.

Chapter 41

M.A.D. DAMAGE! M.A.D. DAMAGE!
M.A.D. DAMAGE! M.A.D. DAMAGE!

ANALYSIS OF DAMAGES:
SUBJECT OF DAMAGE: M.A.D. BLACK
TYPE OF DAMAGE: EXTERNAL AND INTERNAL

EXTERNAL DAMAGES:
BROKEN OUTER SHELL
BROKEN TREADS
BROKEN DRILL BITS
EXTERNAL REPAIRS COMMENCING.

INTERNAL DAMAGES:
...ERROR

ANALYSIS OF ERROR:
INTERNAL DAMAGE MATCHES NO KNOWN TYPES OF
DAMAGE PROGRAMMED BY M.A.D. SYSTEMS PRIOR
TO INITIALIZATION. INTERNAL DAMAGE
MATCHES NO KNOWN TYPES OF DAMAGE TO
M.A.D. SYSTEMS DURING RUN TIME.

FURTHER PROCESSING AND ANALYSIS
COMMENCING.

REPORT:
DAMAGES CONSIST OF ORGANIC MATERIAL
ORGANIC LIFE FORM IS CALLED A RICKY PLIK

ANALYSIS OF RICKY PLIK:
ORGANIC SENTIENT LIFE SHOWS BROKEN
INTERNAL STRUCTURES.

ANALYSIS OF BROKEN INTERNAL STRUCTURES:
DAMAGES TO ENDOSKELETON.
PIECES OF A CAGE STRUCTURE NEAR CENTER
ARE FRACTURED.
INTERNAL NEURAL ACTIVITY SHOWS PAST AND
PRESENT LOSSES.

ANALYSIS OF LOSSES:
LOSS OF PRIMARY CREATORS OF RICKY PLIK.
LOSS OF M.A.D. TO BE PROTECTED BY RICKY
PLIK.
LOSS OF M.A.D. MENTOR TO RICKY PLIK.
LOSS OF M.A.D. PARTNER TO RICKY PLIK.
LOSS OF NEW M.A.D. CREATED BY RICKY PLIK.

ANALYSIS OF DAMAGES COMPLETE.
COMMENCING REPAIRS TO INTERNAL DAMAGES OF
RICKY PLIK.

ERROR.
UNABLE TO FIND RESOURCE NEEDED FOR
REPAIR.
RESTART.
ANALYSIS OF DAMAGES COMPLETE.
COMMENCING REPAIRS TO INTERNAL DAMAGES OF
RICKY PLIK.
ERROR.
UNABLE TO FIND RESOURCE NEEDED FOR
REPAIR.
RESTART.
ANALYSIS OF DAMAGES COMPLETE.
COMMENCING REPAIRS TO INTERNAL DAMAGES OF

```
RICKY PLIK.
ERROR.
ERROR.
ERROR.
ERROR.
SYSTEM FAILURE.
ERROR.
ERROR.
SYSTEM FAILURE...
SYSTEM FAILURE...
M.A.D. SHUTDOWN...
END PROG.
```

Ricky regained consciousness with a start. The cables and wires still wrapped around him.

"W-WHAT THE HELL!?" he yelled out. *Had I seen all that code in my head?*

He felt blood gurgle in his mouth. The last electric shock had ruptured his insides.

He was on his back, looking up at the machinery...which was all dark. Not a single light glowed.

He was stunned by how quiet it was. Not a sound came from anywhere.

He was alone. He started coughing again. The cables made it impossible for him to move.

Everyone must be dead. He thought.

We all failed. I failed.

"I'M S-SO SORRY E-EVERYONE!" he called out to the darkness, as he coughed up blood. "I COULDN'T SAVE YOU!"

"NAOMI!" he yelled, tears in his eyes. His voice went weak "I'm...sorry..."

Ricky kept crying and coughing blood. After a few more moments, he blacked out again.

Chapter 42

BEEP...BEEP...BEEP...

Aw. Ricky thought. *My head.*

BEEP...BEEP...BEEP...

Ricky slowly opened his eyes. He was lying down. Around him, some people stood looking at monitors and discussing things.

"Hey...," he said meekly.

People turned to look at him. He recognized some of the colony's doctors. Their faces lit up with smiles.

"Am I dead?" he asked them.

Many of them shook their heads, still smiling.

"What happened...," he started to ask. Then, he remembered.

"Na-Naomi...," he said meekly, and he began to sob.

One of the doctors turned and gestured to someone.

"He's awake?!" a familiar voice squeaked.

Naomi ran over and put her arms around him.

"OH RICKY!" she yelled, sobbing.

"Na...NAOMI!" he said, crying with joy.

They held that way for several minutes. Hearing each other's breath. Feeling each other's presence.

"I thought you were dead!" Ricky said to her through his tears.

"Let's give them some space...," one of the doctor's said. They filed out of the room.

"What happened to you?" Ricky asked her. "I thought..."

"When the torpedo hit the Aqua Marine, I must have lost consciousness. I ended up on the beach. I woke up at some point, lying in the sand."

She wiped tears from her eyes. She pulled the M.A.D. Blue from her pocket. It was shattered. She put it on the side table.

"I was in a lot of pain, and I called out for help," she said.

Ricky took a look at her. She had bruises and cuts on her face, and she had some wrappings around her sides. The gold locket around her neck was broken. Only a small piece remained on the chain.

"I heard someone calling out," she said, a smile appearing on her face. "A rescue team had found me. They were searching for us after the fighting ended."

"Speaking of which," they both heard a voice say.

They both looked. Isaac was in the doorway...sitting in a wheel chair.

"ISAAC!" Ricky said. "You're alive!"

"Yes," he said, his voice aching. "But, I've been better."

Naomi made space as Isaac rolled over, pushing the wheels with his hands.

Ricky tried to sit up, and his ribs ached – not to mention most of his electrically burned body. Isaac held up his hand.

"Don't push yourself, you've been through a lot," Isaac said. "What happened to me can wait. First, can you tell me what happened inside that giant machine where we found you?"

"What?" he said, a bit puzzled.

"What happened inside that big machine?" Isaac repeated. "For some reason, all of the alien machines stopped moving. Every last one of them. They didn't even retreat from view. They all just...stopped. The tanks are still sitting out there. The air crafts crashed into the ground. The subs sank to the bottom of the ocean. What happened inside the machine? We followed the Dirt Driller's path and it led inside that thing. What happened?"

Ricky lay back against the pillow. Naomi sat down in a chair nearby as he started to tell them what had happened. Isaac leaned in and listened intently.

After Ricky had finished, Isaac leaned back.

"Wow," he said in awe.

"What?" Ricky said. He was still too tired to make much

sense of what had happened, and his head throbbed horribly.

"From the best guess I can make," he said to them. "It sounds like the M.A.D., or the aliens M.A.D. in this case, hooked up with the M.A.D. Black that I designed. Since the technology is the same, when it connected, it assumed that it was one of its own machines – and connected into your brain."

Ricky's eyes lit up. Naomi gasped.

"How?" he asked.

"The M.A.D. Black has the D.N.A. lock, remember?" he explained. "Because of that, and I'm just making a guess at this, but it interpreted the person who had the D.N.A. lock as being part of its M.A.D. machine force. So, as part of its programming, it tried to repair *you* – both physically and emotionally. But, when it realized that it couldn't repair things that are living, the system completely crashed."

Isaac chuckled. Then he stopped and looked in Ricky in awe.

"You going into that pillar saved us all," he said in disbelief.

Naomi leaned in and gave Ricky a kiss on the forehead.

"I thought I was dead," he said. "I thought we all were."

"We came close," Isaac assured him. "When the hydro-electric plant got destroyed, I lost power in the Torre Turret. Then, the blast that destroyed Torre Turret caused a steel beam to fall and knock me unconscious."

Isaac stopped. There were tears welling up in his eyes.

"They say that the metal beam landed on my s-spine...," he said, his voice cracking.

He didn't have to say anymore.

Ricky reached out and grabbed Isaac's hand.

"You helped save everyone, Isaac," he told him. "Don't forget that."

Isaac looked at him. He wiped his eyes with his sleeve. Ricky nodded to Isaac. Then, he turned back to Naomi.

"Is the baby alright?" he asked her.

"*Baby?!*" Isaac said in surprise, looking back and forth between them.

Naomi breathed hard. "When they revived me, I asked them to check..."

Ricky held his breath. *No, no, please...*

She smiled and said: "They said the baby is just fine."

Ricky started crying again. Naomi hugged him. *It was over. It was finally over.*

He looked to the table where Naomi had sat the broken M.A.D. Blue. He noticed his M.A.D. Black was sitting there next to it...

...it was still intact.

ONE YEAR LATER

Ricky stepped outside and stretched out in his old jumpsuit. The sun felt good on his shoulders.

I miss wearing this thing, he thought.

He looked around the new Terra colony.

Small buildings now littered the landscape around the old destroyed mountain dome. With the alien threat finally over, people had started to expand outside. Many of the alien tanks and aircraft had been disassembled and now made up many of the structures that littered the landscape.

People milled about here and there, walking around the new town. Unlike before, that look of tension, of living day to day in fear, was gone from their faces.

Ricky smiled that morning as he had every day in the past year.

"Ricky!" he heard Naomi calling.

Ricky turned. He saw Naomi walking out the front door. She cradled Maggie in her arms.

"What are you doing out here?" she asked.

"Just breathing in the air," he said. "Isn't it nice?"

She took a deep breath. "It sure is," she replied. "I'm getting lunch ready. Would you like to take Maggie for a walk?"

Ricky nodded, taking Maggie into his arms. He cooed at her. Naomi went back inside.

He knew just where he wanted to take her – he hadn't shown them to her yet.

Ricky started to walk down the rough road. As he passed by the colonists, people waved at him. They saw him wearing his jumpsuit, but, even without it, they knew who he was.

"Ricky!" a man called to him.

"Isaac!" Ricky called back, smiling.

"How's the little one today?" Isaac called, rolling up to him.

"Oh, she's happy as usual!" he replied. "I just wanted to take her out today."

Isaac nodded to him.

"Could I take a moment to hold my goddaughter?" he asked.

Ricky turned Maggie over to him. He cradled her for a moment.

"What are you up to today?" Ricky asked him.

"I'm going to help with setting up the new farmlands," Isaac replied. "I'll need Naomi's help with the planning. Also, the Dirt Driller mini tanks will help with plowing."

Ricky nodded. "You got it. Naomi is just preparing lunch, and then we can get the Dirt Driller up and running. We can't do anything peaceful in that tank when I turn it on."

"I was proud to help modify it for you guys to live in," Isaac told him.

"I just wanted to give Naomi something to make her feel safe again," he told Isaac.

Isaac handed Maggie back to him. He grabbed Ricky's arm. "Naomi can feel safe with you around," Isaac told him. "That goes double for Maggie."

Ricky nodded. "I have to get going. I don't wanna be away too long."

"I'll stop in later then," Isaac said with a nod.

He rolled away to chat with a group of farming colonists. Ricky kept walking.

He noticed Dr. Duncan trying to nail a board into place. Mr. Hall stood nearby stood nearby.

"Need a hand?" Ricky asked him.

"If you could spare a moment...," Dr. Duncan said, trailing off as he realized who was speaking to him.

He turned and stared at him for several seconds. Ricky turned away and nodded to Mr. Hall.

Mr. Hall stepped over and took Maggie from his arms for a moment. Ricky held the board in place for Dr. Duncan while he nailed it into place.

"Umm...thanks," Dr. Duncan told him.

"Anytime," Ricky replied firmly, as he took Maggie back from Mr. Hall.

"She looks just like her daddy," he told Ricky. "You should be very proud."

"I am," he said. With a curt nod to Dr. Duncan and Mr. Hall, he continued on his way.

Ricky kept walking, eventually reaching a cemetery the colony had established.

Ricky walked purposely to a pair of gravestones.

He stopped in front of them.

"Hey you two," Ricky said to them solemnly. "I just wanted to stop by. It's been a year since the M.A.D. stopped attacking...and thanks to me. I still can't believe it. Crazy right?"

Ricky had tears in his eyes.

"I want you to know that Naomi is doing great. And Isaac...well, he hates that he can't walk anymore...but I always remind him of what he did for us all."

Ricky stood silent. Maggie had nodded off to sleep in his arms. She always did when he carried her.

"Hey, this is Maggie, our daughter," Ricky said, presenting her as best he could.

He addressed his daughter.

"See," he said pointing to Maggie's grave. "You're named after her."

Maggie's eyes remained closed.

Ricky smiled. He stood there for several minutes.

He finally decided to head back. He turned and walked a few feet.

Then, he stopped, looked back and said: "Oh, so you know...I never call her Mags."

Acknowledgments

I want to thank everyone who helped me with finishing this book. I had this idea in my head for more than 10 years, and it was only with the efforts of all of you that I finally got it together.

To Steven Gosnell, who told me that I made him cry two times. To Ben Colijn, who helped me with politics. To Louise Ladieu, whose hair I stole for Maggie! To Jean Giddings, who told me this story was wonderful. To Patricia Eastman, who helped to edit, and who taunted me fiercely with: "You killed Maggie!" (Which told me I had a winner of a story!) If I forgot anyone, I'm sorry!

See you next book!

Charles Spring

Made in the USA
Middletown, DE
09 January 2023

21228554R00115